2-15-20

FLOWER CHILDREN

ALSO BY MAXINE SWANN

Serious Girls: A Novel

FLOWER CHILDREN

Maxine Swann

RIVERHEAD BOOKS

a member of Penguin Group (USA) Inc.

New York ✳ *2007*

RIVERHEAD BOOKS
Published by the Penguin Group
Penguin Group (USA) Inc., 375 Hudson Street, New York, New York 10014, USA ●
Penguin Group (Canada), 90 Eglinton Avenue East, Suite 700, Toronto, Ontario M4P 2Y3,
Canada (a division of Pearson Penguin Canada Inc.) ● Penguin Books Ltd, 80 Strand,
London WC2R 0RL, England ● Penguin Ireland, 25 St Stephen's Green, Dublin 2, Ireland
(a division of Penguin Books Ltd) ● Penguin Group (Australia), 250 Camberwell Road,
Camberwell, Victoria 3124, Australia (a division of Pearson Australia Group Pty Ltd) ●
Penguin Books India Pvt Ltd, 11 Community Centre, Panchsheel Park, New Delhi–110 017,
India ● Penguin Group (NZ), 67 Apollo Drive, Mairangi Bay, Auckland 1311, New Zealand
(a division of Pearson New Zealand Ltd) ● Penguin Books (South Africa) (Pty) Ltd,
24 Sturdee Avenue, Rosebank, Johannesburg 2196, South Africa

Penguin Books Ltd, Registered Offices: 80 Strand, London WC2R 0RL, England

Some of these stories appeared, in different form, in *The Best American Short Stories* (1998 and
2006), *The O. Henry Prize Stories* (1998), *Open City, Ploughshares,* and *The Pushcart Prize XXII.*

Library of Congress Cataloging-in-Publication Data

Swann, Maxine.
Flower children / Maxine Swann.
p.   cm.
ISBN 978-1-59448-945-7
1. Hippies—Family relationships—Fiction.   2. United States—History–1969—Fiction.
I. Title.

PS3619.W356F55   2007   2006039269
813'.6—dc22

Printed in the United States of America
1   3   5   7   9   10   8   6   4   2

Book design by Meighan Cavanaugh

For my mother and father
and my siblings, Leda, Jake, and Kyle

Contents

*

FLOWER CHILDREN

They're free to run anywhere they like whenever they like, so they do. The land falls away from their small house on the hill along a prickly path; there's a dirt road, a pasture where the steer are kept, swamps, a gully, groves of fruit trees, and then the creek from whose far bank a wooded mountain surges—they climb it. At the top, they step out to catch their breaths in the light. The mountain gives way into fields as far as their eyes can see—alfalfa, soybean, corn, wheat. They aren't sure where their own land stops and someone else's begins, but it doesn't matter, they're told: It doesn't matter! Go where you please!

They spend their whole lives in trees, young apple trees and old tired ones, red oaks, walnuts, the dogwood when it flowers in May. They hold leaves up to the light and peer through them. They close their eyes and press their faces into showers of leaves and wait for that feeling of darkness to come and make their whole bodies stir. They discover locust shells, tree frogs, a gypsy moth's cocoon. Now they know what that sound is in the night when the tree frogs sing out at the tops of their lungs. In the fields, they collect groundhog bones. They make desert piles and bless them with flowers and leaves. They wish they could be plants and lie very still near the ground all night and in the morning be covered with tears of dew. They wish they could be Robin Hood, Indians. In the summer, they rub mud all over their bodies and sit out in the sun to let it dry. When it dries, they stand up slowly like old men and women with wrinkled skin and walk stiff-limbed through the trees toward the creek.

Their parents don't care what they do. They're the luckiest children alive! They run out naked in storms. They take baths with their father, five bodies in one tub. In the pasture, they stretch out flat on their backs and wait for the buzzards to come. When the buzzards start circling, they lie very still, breathless with fear, and imagine what it would be like to be eaten alive. That one's diving! they say, and they leap to their feet: No, we're alive! We're alive!

The children all sleep in one room. Their parents built the house themselves, four rooms and four stories high, one small room on top of the next. With their first child, a girl, they lived out in a tent in the yard beneath the apple trees. In the children's room, there are three beds. The girls sleep together, and the youngest boy in a wooden crib their mother made. A toilet stands out in the open near the stairwell. Their parents sleep on the highest floor underneath the eaves in a room with skylights and silver-papered walls. In the living room, a swing hangs in the center from the ceiling. There's a woodstove to one side with a bathtub beside it; both the bathtub and the stove stand on lion's feet. There are bookshelves all along the walls and an atlas, too, which the children pore through, and a set of encyclopedias from which they copy fish. The kitchen, the lowest room, is built into a hill. The floor is made of dirt and gravel and the stone walls are damp. Blacksnakes come in sometimes to shed their skins. When the children aren't outside, they spend most of their time here; they play with the stones on the floor, making pyramids or round piles and then knocking them down. There's a shower house outside down a steep, narrow path and a round stone well in the woods behind.

There's nowhere to hide in the house, no cellars or

closets, so the children go outside to do that too. They spend hours standing waist-high in the creek. They watch the crayfish have battles and tear off each other's claws. They catch the weak ones later, off guard and from behind, as they crouch in the dark under shelves of stone. And they catch minnows, too, and salamanders with the soft skin of frogs, and they try to catch snakes although they're never quite sure that they really want to. It maddens them how the water changes things before their eyes, turning the minnows into darting chips of green light and making the dirty stones on the bottom shine. Once they found a snapping turtle frozen in the ice and their father cut it out with an ax to make soup. The children dunk their heads under and breathe out bubbles. They keep their heads down as long as they can. They like how their hair looks underneath the water, the way it spreads out around their faces in wavering fans. And their voices sound different, too, like the voices of strange people from a foreign place. They put their heads down and carry on conversations, they scream and laugh, testing out these strange voices that bloom from their mouths and then swell outward, endlessly, like no other sound they have ever heard.

The children get stung by nettles, ants, poison ivy, poison oak, and bees. They go out into the swamp and come back, their whole heads crawling with ticks and burrs. They pick one another's scalp outside the house, then lay the ticks on a ledge and grind their bodies to dust with a pointed stone.

They watch the pigs get butchered and the chickens killed. They learn that people have teeth inside their heads. One evening, their father takes his shirt off and lies out on the kitchen table to show them where their organs are. He moves his hand over the freckled skin, cupping different places—heart, stomach, lung, lung, kidneys, gallbladder, liver here. And suddenly they want to know what's inside everything, so they tear apart everything they find, flowers, pods, bugs, shells, seeds, they shred up the whole yard in search of something; and they want to know about everything they see or can't see, frost and earthworms, and who will decide when it rains, and are there ghosts and are there fairies, and how many drops and how many stars, and although they kill things themselves, they want to know why anything dies and where the dead go and where they were waiting before they were born. In the hazelnut grove?

Behind the goat house? And how did they know when it was time to come?

Their parents are delighted by the snow lady they build with huge breasts and a penis and rock-necklace hair. Their parents are delighted by these children in every way, these children who will be like no children ever were. In this house with their children, they'll create a new world—one that has no relation to the world they have known—in which nothing is lied about, whispered about, and nothing is ever concealed. There will be no petty lessons for these children about how a fork is held or a hand shaken or what is best to be said and what shouldn't be spoken of or seen. Nor will these children's minds be restricted to sets and subsets of rules, rules for children, about when to be quiet or go to bed, the causes and effects of various punishments that increase in gravity on a gradated scale. No, not these children! These children will be different. They'll learn only the large things. Here in this house, the world will be revealed in a fresh, new light and this light will fall over everything. Even those shady forbidden zones through which they themselves wandered as children, panicked and alone: these, too, will be illuminated—their children will walk through with torches held high! Yes, everything should be spoken of in this house, everything, and everything seen.

＊

Their father holds them on his lap when he's going to the bathroom, he lights his farts with matches on the stairs, he likes to talk about shit and examine each shit he takes, its texture and smell, and the children's shits, too, he has theories about shit that unwind for hours—he has theories about everything. He has a study in the toolshed near the house where he sits for hours and is visited regularly by ideas that he comes in to explain to their mother and the children. When their mother's busy or not listening, he explains them to the children or to only one child in a language that they don't understand, but certain words or combinations of words bore themselves into their brains where they will remain, but the children don't know this yet, ringing in their ears for the rest of their lives—Nixon, wind power, nuclear power, Vietnam, fecal patterns, sea thermal energy, the est training, civil rights. And one day these words will bear all sorts of meaning, but now they mean nothing to the children—they live the lives of ghosts, outlines with no form, wandering inside their minds. The children listen attentively. They nod, nod, nod.

Their parents grow pot in the garden that they keep under the kitchen sink in a large tin. When the babysitter comes, their mother shows her where it is. The babysitter plays with the children, a game where you turn the music up very loud and run around the living room leaping from the couch to the chairs to the swing, trying never to touch the floor. She shows them the tattoo between her legs, a bright rose with thorns, and then she calls up all her friends. When the children come down later to get juice in the kitchen, they see ten naked bodies through a cloud of smoke sitting around the table, playing cards. The children are invited, but they'd rather not play.

Their parents take them to protests in different cities and to concerts sometimes. The children wear T-shirts and hold posters and then the whole crowd lets off balloons. Their parents have peach parties and invite all their friends. There's music, dancing, skinny-dipping in the creek. Everyone takes off their clothes and rubs peach flesh all over each other's skin. The children are free to join in but they don't feel like it. They sit in a row on the hill in all their clothes.

But they memorize the sizes of the breasts and the shapes of the penises of all their parents' friends and discuss this later among themselves.

One day, at the end of winter, a woman begins to come to their house. She has gray eyes and a huge mound of wheat-colored hair. She laughs quickly, showing small white teeth. From certain angles, she looks ugly, but from others she seems very nice. She comes in the mornings and picks things in the garden. She's there again at dinner, at birthdays. She brings presents. She arrives dressed as a rabbit for Easter in a bright yellow pajama suit. She's very kind to their mother and chatters to her for hours in the kitchen as they cook. Their father goes away on weekends with her; he spends the night at her house. Sometimes he takes the children with him to see her. She lives in a gray house by the river that's much larger than the children's house. She has six Siamese cats. She has a piano and many records and piles of soft clay for the children to play with but they don't want to. They go outside and stand by the concrete frog pond near the road. Algae covers it like a hairy, green blanket. They stare down, trying to spot frogs. They chuck rocks in, candy, pennies, or whatever else they can find.

In the gray spring mornings, there's a man either coming or going from their mother's room. He leaves the door open. Did you hear them? I heard them. Did you see them? Yes. But they don't talk about it. They no longer talk about things among themselves. But they answer their father's questions when he asks.

And here again they nod. When their father has gone away for good and then comes back to visit or takes them out on trips in his car and tells them about the women he's been with, how they make love, what he prefers or doesn't like, gestures or movements of the arms, neck, or legs described in the most detailed terms: And what do they think? And what would they suggest? When a woman stands with a cigarette between her breasts at the end of the bed and you suddenly lose all hope. And he talks about their mother, too, the way she makes love. He'd much rather talk to them than to anyone else. These children, they're amazing! They rise to all occasions, stoop carefully to any sorrow—and their minds! Their minds are wide open and flow with no stops, like damless streams. And the children nod also when one of their mother's boyfriends comes by to see her—she's not there—they're often heartbroken, occasionally drunk, they want to talk about her. The children stand with them underneath the trees. They can't see for the sun in their eyes but they look up anyway and nod, smile politely, nod.

The children play with their mother's boyfriends out in the snow. They go to school. They're sure they'll never learn to read. They stare at the letters. They lose all hope. They worry that they don't know the Lord's Prayer. They realize that they don't know God or anything about Him, so they ask the other children shy questions in the schoolyard and receive answers that baffle them, and then God fills their minds like a guest who's moved in, but keeps his distance, and worries them to distraction at night when they're alone. They imagine they hear his movements through the house, his footsteps and the rustling of his clothes. They grow frightened for their parents, who seem to have learned nothing about God's laws. They feel that they should warn them but they don't know how. They become convinced one night that their mother is a robber. They hear her creeping through the house alone, lifting and rattling things.

At school, they learn to read and spell. They learn penmanship and multiplication. They're surprised at first by all the rules, but then they learn them too quickly and observe them all carefully. They learn not to swear. They get prizes for obedience, for following the rules down to the last detail. They're delighted by these rules, these arbitrary lines that regulate behavior and mark off forbidden things and they examine them closely and exhaust their teachers with questions about the mechanical functioning and the hidden intricacies of these beings, the rules: If at naptime, you're very quiet with your eyes shut tight and your arms and legs so still you barely breathe, but really you're not sleeping, underneath your arms and beneath your eyelids you're wide awake and thinking very hard about how to be still, but you get the prize anyway for sleeping because you were the stillest child in the room, but actually that's wrong, you shouldn't get the prize or should you, because the prize is really for sleeping and not being still, or is it also for being still . . . ?

When the other children in the schoolyard are whispering themselves into wild confusion about their bodies and sex and babies being born, these children stay quiet and stand to one side. They're mortified by what they know and have seen. They're sure that if they mention one word, the other children will go home and tell their parents who will tell their teachers who will be horrified and disgusted and push them away. But they also think they should be punished. They should be shaken, beaten, for what they've seen. These children don't touch themselves. They grow hesitant with worry. At home, they wander out into the yard alone and stand there at a terrible loss. One day, when the teacher calls on them, they're no longer able to speak. But then they speak again a few days later, although now and then they'll have periods in their lives when their voices disappear utterly or else become very thin and quavering like ghosts or old people lost in their throats.

But the children love to read. They suddenly discover the use of all these books in the house and turn the living room into a lending library. Each book has a card and a due date and is stamped when it's borrowed or returned. They play card games and backgammon. They go over to friends' houses and learn about junk food and how to watch TV. But mostly they read. They read about anything, love stories, the lives of inventors and famous Indians, blights that affect hybrid plants. They try to read books they can't read at all and skip words and whole paragraphs and sit like this for hours lost in a stunning blur.

They take violin lessons at school and piano lessons and then stop one day when their hands begin to shake so badly they can no longer hold to the keys. What is wrong? Nothing! They get dressed up in costumes and put on plays. They're kings and queens. They're witches. They put on a whole production of *The Wizard of Oz*. They play detectives with identity cards and go searching for the kittens who have just been born in some dark, hidden place on their land. They store away money to give to their father when he comes. They spend whole afternoons at the edge of the yard waiting for him to come. They don't understand why their father behaves so strangely now, why he sleeps in their mother's bed when she's gone in the afternoon and then gets up and slinks around the house, like a criminal, chuckling, especially when she's angry and has told him to leave. They don't know why their father seems laughed at now and unloved, why he needs money from them to drive home in his car, why he seems to need something from them that they cannot give him—everything, but they'll try to give him—everything—whatever it is he needs, they'll try to do this as hard as they can.

Their father comes and waits for their mother in the house. He comes and takes them away on trips in his car. They go to quarries where they line up and leap off cliffs. They go looking for caves up in the hills in Virginia.

There are bears here, he tells them, but if you ever come face-to-face with one, just swear your heart out and he'll run. He takes them to dances in the city where only old people go: Don't they know how to foxtrot? Don't they know how to waltz? They sit at tables and order sodas, waiting for their turn to be picked up and whirled around by him. Or they watch him going around to other tables, greeting husbands and inviting their wives, women much older than his mother, to dance. These women have blue or white hair. They either get up laughing or refuse. He comes back to the children to report how they were—like dancing with milk, he says, or water, or molasses. He takes them to see the pro wrestling championship match. He takes them up north for a week to meditate inside a hotel with a guru from Bombay. He takes them running down the up escalators in stores and up Totem Mountain at night in a storm. He talks his head off. He gets speeding tickets left and right. He holds them on his lap when he's driving and between his legs when they ski. When he begins to fall asleep at the wheel, they rack their brains, trying to think of ways to keep him awake. They rub his shoulders and pull his hair. They sing rounds. They ask him questions to try to make him talk. They do interviews in the backseat, saying things they know will amuse him. And when their efforts are exhausted, he tells them that the only way he'll ever stay awake is if they insult him in the cruelest way they can. He says their mother is the only person who can do this really well. He tells them that they have to say mean things about her, about her boyfriends and lovers and what they do, or about how much she hates him, thinks he's stupid, an asshole, a failure, how much she doesn't want him around. And so they do. They force themselves to invent insults or say things that are terrible but true. And as they speak, they feel their mouths turn chalky and their stomachs begin to harden as if with each word they had swallowed a stone. But he seems delighted. He laughs and encourages them, turning around in his seat to look at their faces, his eyes now completely off the road.

He wants them to meet everyone he knows. They show up on people's doorsteps with him in the middle of the day or late at night. He can hardly contain himself. These are my kids! he says. They're smarter than anyone I know, and ten times smarter than me! Do you have any idea what it's like when your kids turn out smarter than you?! He teaches them how to play bridge and to ski backward. At dinner with him, you have to eat with your eyes closed. When you go through a stoplight, you have to hold on to your balls. But the girls? Oh yes, the girls—well, just improvise! He's experiencing flatulence, withdrawal from wheat. He's on a new diet that will ruthlessly clean out his bowels. There are turkeys and assholes everywhere in the world. Do they know this? Do they know? But he himself is probably the biggest asshole here. Still, women find him handsome— they do! They actually do! And funny. But he *is* funny, he actually *is,* not witty but funny, they don't realize this because they see him all the time, they're used to it, but other people—like that waitress! Did they see that waitress? She was laughing so hard she could barely see straight! Do they know how you get to be a waitress? Big breasts. But he himself is not a breast man. Think of Mom—he calls their mother Mom—she has no breasts at all! But her taste in men is mind-boggling. Don't they think? Mind-boggling! Think about it too long and you'll lose your mind. Why do they think she picks these guys? What is it? And why are women almost always so much smarter than men? And more dignified? Dignity for men is a completely lost cause! And why does anyone have kids anyway? Come on, why?! Because they like you? Because they laugh at you? No! Because they're fun! Exactly! They're fun!

*

Around the house there are briar patches with berries and thorns. There are gnarled apple trees with puckered gray skins. The windows are all open—the wasps are flying in. The clothes on the line are jumping like children with no heads but hysterical limbs. Who will drown the fresh new kitties? Who will chainsaw the trees and cut the firewood in winter and haul that firewood in? Who will do away with all these animals, or tend them, or sell them, kill them one by one? Who will say to her in the evening that it all means nothing, that tomorrow will be different, that the heart gets tired after all? And where are the children? When will they come home? She has burned all her diaries. She has told the man in the barn to go away. Who will remind her again that the heart has its own misunderstandings? And the heart often loses its way and can be found hours later wandering down passageways with unexplained bruises on its skin. On the roof, there was a child standing one day years ago, his arms waving free but one foot turned inward, weakly. When will it be evening? When will it be night? The tree frogs are beginning to sing. She has seen the way their toes clutch at the bark. Some of them are spotted, and their hearts beat madly against the skin of their throats. There may be a storm. It may rain. That cloud there looks dark—but no, it's a wisp of burned paper, too thin. In the woods above, there's a house that burned down to the ground, but then a grove of lilac bushes burst up from the char. A wind is coming up. There are dark purple clouds now. There are red-coned sumacs hovering along the edge of the drive. Poisonous raw, but fine for tea. The leaves on the apple trees are all turning blue. The sunflowers in the garden are quivering, heads bowed—empty of seed now. And the heart gets watered and recovers itself. There is hope, everywhere there's hope. Light approaches from the back. Between the dry, gnarled branches, it's impossible to see. There are the first few drops. There are the oak trees shuddering. There's a flicker of bright gray, the underside of one leaf. There was once a child standing at the edge of the yard at a terrible loss. Did she know this? Yes. The children! (They have her arms, his ears, his voice, his smell, her soft features, her movements of the hand and head, her stiffness, his confusion, his humor, her ambition, his daring, his eyelids, their failure, their hope, their freckled skin . . .)

THE OUTLAWS

At hunting season, the hunters always came onto our land, though our mother put up No Hunting signs. We'd hear shots in the day. Our mother told us not to walk around much, or if we did, to wear orange or red. At night, along our usually quiet dirt road, there'd be sounds of trucks peeling out and drunken voices. Other times of the year, there'd sometimes be a collection of people down in the woods by their cars drinking beer, or else they'd slip into the swimming hole. You could always tell when some-one had been there, from the way the sand looked or be-cause they'd left things behind, a T-shirt, a beer can.

It was the fall after our father had left that they shot the dogs. Sometimes our dogs had come home wounded—the neighbor had taken a rough shot at one of them for chasing his sheep, or they'd gotten into a fight with the wild dog pack. Some evenings they wouldn't come home at all. But this time they'd been missing for days.

Our mother's boyfriend, Bobby, found them up in the fields, three of them, shot dead, Henry Gray, Jenny, and the stray. He piled them onto the back of his pickup and brought them down to the house, where he laid their bodies out on the grass. Tuck and I were coming up from the creek—we'd been checking to see if it was frozen—so were the first to see. Henry Gray's mouth was open and you could see all his teeth. Jenny's blonder fur was spattered with blood. Polly, the stray, a black Lab mutt with one blue eye, had been shot in the chest. Bobby was kneeling down, stroking Polly's head. He had had a black Lab himself who had died not long ago.

Tuck, five, stared at the dogs. He looked bewildered. His fat cheeks burned. Our mother was walking up from the wood pile. When she saw the dogs, she paused, then kept walking, her face growing dimmer as she arrived. Clyde trailed behind her. He was wearing his cowboy clothes, a hat and spurs, and carrying a metal pistol. The littlest, three, he was already a loudmouth.

"What's *wrong* with them?" he asked, once he arrived, poking at Jenny's leg with his pistol.

Lu drifted over. Bundled up, she'd been doing ballet movements by the shriveled herb garden. She was the oldest, nine. We were all of us two years apart, Lu, then me, then Tuck and Clyde. At seven, I was stocky and strong. Lu had a mole on her cheek and always carried her head tilted to one side. Now she gazed for a moment at the dogs, then, letting out a high, soft sob, turned abruptly and ran toward the house. Her limbs were loose and springy; you could see, as she ran, the bottoms of her shoes.

Our mother knelt down on the grass beside Bobby. She had full lips, a cloud of dark hair. "Where did you find them?" she asked.

"In the soybeans," Bobby said, "right above the beaver pond." He'd been up there to cut firewood.

It was still strange having him around. For years he'd been a figure at protests and parties, standing by the band, jiggling his foot. He liked to dance, to go skinny-dipping. After our father left, he started coming around. Younger than our mother by seven years, he worked as a trucker and had his own Mack truck. He and our mother went off on a road trip together, to New Mexico, and brought us back bear-claw rings. Then one night in February, in the middle of an ice storm, he'd showed up at our house on his chestnut horse, Jack. The roads were too icy to drive. Bobby had a broken leg: on the ride over, Jack had slipped and fallen on it. But he'd kept going because he'd had to go somewhere. His house had just burned down to the ground.

After that, he moved in with us—"for a while," our mother said. I didn't like the way he acted, as if he were here to stay. But Lu didn't seem to mind. He'd turn the music up very loud, Waylon Jennings, "The Outlaws," and try to get us to dance. I wouldn't, but Lu would, and so would our mother, Bobby wiggling his hips, our mother following along, stepping out of tune.

But now he was angry. He banged the back of the pickup closed. "I'm going to find that motherfucker," he said. We watched him drive away, Clyde standing, feet apart, twirling his pistol.

When Bobby returned that night, it was already dark. He buried the dogs in the pasture and then came up to the house. I heard him and our mother talking downstairs.

"I found out who it was: Martin McClure. They say he's been bragging around town. We'll go over there tomorrow, take the kids after school."

"You think we should bring the kids?" our mother asked. "He has to see the kids," Bobby said.

✳

Our school was a low brick building with a flag out front and a playground behind. In the halls there was a yellowish light. From the classrooms, you could look out and see the cars in the parking lot or a wavering patch of grass.

All the teachers were old and wore floral dresses and different shades of perfume, except for our principal, Miss Vaught, who dressed in full skirts, high heels and pantyhose, like a saloon girl. In the mornings we said the Pledge of Allegiance and then the Lord's Prayer. There was a library with a card catalogue and low shelves lined with biographies of American heroes, Benjamin Franklin, Davy Crockett, Chief Sitting Bull. The dining hall was furnished with linoleum tables with similar benches attached. We had hot meals on trays with depressed surfaces in them, each to hold a portion of something. The women who worked in the dining hall wore nets over their hair.

At recess, we went outside and played on the tarmac or on the grassy field below, kickball, dodgeball. The girls who wore pretty dresses didn't always play. They stood against the brick wall talking instead. Martin McClure's sister, Christina, was one of these. She had long spindly legs and straight blue-black hair. I had gone once to a birthday party at her house. Her brother, Martin, much older than us, with the same sleek blue-black hair, had been there. Her mother ran an in-house beauty salon. The beauty parlor chair had been in the living room, with all kinds of bottles and sprays scattered around. The day after our dogs were shot, I eyed Christina nervously. I wondered what she'd heard, if she'd heard anything. I knew we'd be going to her house after school.

At school, we felt funny and kept our heads down. Mostly everyone else went to church, except maybe the Ballards, whose clothes were always dirty and whose father made moonshine. There was also the Amish family who lived on the bus route. They lived in their own way entirely and didn't even go to school. But everyone else, it seemed, had TVs in their house, and guns, and in the fall went hunting, and their parents dressed up for parents' meetings.

There was only one other girl in my class whose parents were like our parents, and friends with them. Like us, she had a trapeze in her living room. Her parents were both painters, at all the parties. Her mother wore transparent blouses to school.

In school we kept up a wary friendship. We knew secrets about each other. Above all, we wanted to fit in.

*

After school, Bobby came by in his pickup and drove us over to the McClures' house.

The McClures' house had a porch up on stilts. There were a bunch of old cars in the yard, some jacked up, someone working on them, and then smaller structures around, sheds, a half-open awning with a lawn mower under it. Behind a fence, a horse, looking bedraggled, tipped its head down to lick a salt block.

As we nosed in the driveway between other cars—there were quite a few cars—Martin McClure himself came out of the house. He was very handsome, as I remembered, and dressed now to go out. He had lace-up shoes with heels on them, tan polyester pants, a velour V-neck. We kids, bundled up, were sitting in the back of the pickup. Our mother and Bobby climbed out of the cab.

"You Martin?" Bobby asked.

"Yeah," Martin said, already cocking his chin. I hoped Christina wasn't watching. Then I saw her face in the window.

"You killed those dogs, didn't you?" Bobby said.

Martin glanced to the side. "What dogs?"

"These kids' dogs, you killed them."

Martin looked at us, chin still lifted, then away.

Bobby stepped up nearer to Martin. "We heard you been bragging around town about it."

Martin looked at Bobby defiantly. With his high heels on, he was much taller. Bobby was compact, roly-poly. Now he went toward Martin, pressing a finger into his chest.

"What the fuck d'you think you're doing, shooting at dogs?"

"Hey," our mother murmured, looking stiff, uneasy.

The horse glanced up lazily, then stayed there watching. I couldn't bear to look at Christina's face in the window. Instead I kept my eyes on Martin. His cheeks were flushed.

"Get your hands off me," he said nervously, knocking Bobby's finger away.

Tuck gripped Lu's sleeve. Clyde stood up as if he wanted part of the action.

Bobby approached Martin again, pointing his finger. "I want you to say you're sorry," he said. "I want you to look right at these kids and say you're sorry you shot their dogs."

Martin turned and stalked back into the house.

"Where's he going?" Clyde asked, jumping up, excited.

"Come back here. Hey, come back here, asshole!" Bobby said.

I saw Christina's face disappear.

"Okay, it's all right," our mother said.

"Are you fucking crazy?" Bobby said, looking at her. "It's not all right."

Then suddenly Martin came out of the house again, walking fast this time. He headed toward one of the trucks in the drive, raised up high on its wheels.

"Get out of my way, man," he said when Bobby came toward him again.

Christina's face reappeared in the window.

"Just tell me one thing, did you shoot those dogs?"

"Look, man, they were chasing deer. If they're chasing deer, it's legal to shoot."

Bobby swung at Martin. He missed, then swung again and hit him. Clyde jumped up, imitating a punch. Martin, at the blow, backed up, then stumbled back. He was down on the ground, supporting himself with his arms. He put a hand up to his mouth.

Bobby was standing over him. "It's legal to shoot if they're chasing livestock. You know what livestock are? Cows, sheep, that horse you got there, not wild animals."

Martin snickered a little. Now, since the thing had happened—he had been hit—he was looking less scared. "What's wrong with you, man?" he said from down on the ground. "I thought it was all peace and love with you people."

Christina's mother appeared in the doorway. "Martin," she called.

"It's okay, Mom," he said.

Martin got up slowly, cautiously, his eye on Bobby the whole way, as if Bobby were a crazy animal.

"Peace and love and drugs," Martin said, his hand still on his jaw. "Now *that* shit's not legal."

But it seemed clear that Bobby didn't feel like fighting anymore. "I'd watch out for your boy here," he said to Martin's mother, and then he turned and climbed in the truck.

We drove home. There were far round hills with shreds of crops on them, corn husks, stubs of wheat. The trees made spindly spider lines against the sky.

＊

There were shots that evening, muffled ones and then others very near, more hunters on our land. We were in the kitchen, eating dinner, the wagon wheel light above our heads, the pitch dark outside. For a moment, it felt like we were hunkered down, under ambush. When more near shots came, just after dinner, Bobby stood up and, in one movement, pulled on his coat and was out the door.

"Be careful," our mother called after him.

We heard the pickup tear away.

When Bobby came back, a bit later, his mood had changed. His eyes were lit. "Didn't find them," he said, "but I have a plan." We kids were already in our night-clothes. "The kids should get dressed," he said. "We're all going out."

"We are?" Lu asked.

We tramped up the stairs, Tuck and I racing each other. In the bedroom we all shared, we took our pajamas off.

"What are we *doing*?" Clyde asked. Shirt still off, he put his holster back on over his pants.

"We'll have to see," Lu said, sounding like our mother, helping him hook it on.

Outside, it was very dark, the air lined with ice. Our mother was waiting with flashlights by the herb garden. She gave one to Lu and one to me and kept one herself. Up above, Bobby had the tractor headlights on. We headed toward them.

Bobby had hitched the manure spreader up to the tractor. We climbed in. He put the chain saw in there with us and a coil of rope, then leapt on the tractor. Our mother stood with him on the little ledge along the side. Our eyes were adjusting, even with the flashlights out of the way, things looking fuzzy gray now instead of black. Our mother looked back at us.

"Everyone hold on," she said.

Bobby started the tractor. He turned left out the drive. The road this way led through the woods past the fork and then farther, out into the open, cutting through neighbors' fields, ending in the crossroads where the bus stop was. It was a dirt road, narrow, with deep ruts, making for a bumpy ride. As we drove, Tuck, who loved tools, kept one hand on the chain saw. Lu held on to the edge of the manure spreader, gripping Clyde with the other hand. The road got darker through the trees. We passed the fallen corncrib. Near the edge of the tree line, Bobby stopped the tractor.

"Okay," he called back, "everyone down."

Our mother came around and one by one helped us down. Bobby took the chain saw and the rope out of the back.

"You kids stand back. Back, back further," he said, motioning backward with his hand.

We backed up along the road, Lu and me shining the flashlights in front of us. Our mother joined Bobby who, chain saw in hand, was examining the trees by the side of the road. The trees were black and bare, shorn of leaves.

"What are they *doing*?" Clyde asked, jumping up, so that his pistol fell from its holster.

"They're going to cut a tree," Tuck whispered.

"Why?" Clyde asked.

"Shh," Lu said, whispering too. We felt for some reason that we had to be quiet, as if this were an undercover operation.

Bobby hooked one end of the rope over the upper branches of a tree. We followed him with our flashlights. He tied the other end to the tractor.

There was a faint gunshot in the distance, then, behind us in the woods, very near, a crackling sound, branches breaking, something bounding. Lu and I whirled our flashlights around. We peered into the trees, but whatever it had been, an animal of some kind, had already disappeared.

The roar of the chain saw made us jump and turn back. We trained our flashlights on Bobby again. Our mother had her flashlight fixed on Bobby, too, not on his face but his hands holding the saw. He was wearing goggles and dark leather gloves. Bent over, he was cutting a notch into the side of a tree that faced the road.

Farther up the road, a neighbor's light went on. It lit up the far field. Bobby paused, the sound of the chain saw lifting momentarily, then went on cutting. He was now cutting a larger, higher notch into the other side of the tree. The neighbor's light stayed on for a while, then went out, plunging the field back in darkness.

"I have to pee," Clyde said.

"Go over there," Lu said. She pointed her flashlight to the side of the road. "Here, I'll light you."

Clyde stepped over to the side of the road. Tuck went with him and started to pee too. As always, when they peed, I felt I had to. I squatted down in the road behind them.

The chain saw went off. There was silence, then a groaning sound.

"I think it's falling," Lu hissed. We zipped our pants up quickly and went to look. The place where our mother and Bobby had been was empty. Then suddenly, out of the darkness, something dropped, careening. We tried to follow it as it fell, and landed, thudding, an explosion of branches snapping and shattering, then bouncing and settling, straight across the road.

"See?" our mother said, stepping out of the woods, coming toward us, her voice uncharacteristically bright. "Now the hunters won't be able to come onto our land."

"Not bad, eh?" Bobby said, arriving behind her.

Clyde ran over to the fallen tree. He climbed on top of it, straddling it. Tuck asked for my flashlight and went around to examine the cut. Bobby went with him.

"See, you gotta do it that way," Bobby said. "Not straight across."

Tuck stared, satisfied.

"Okay," Bobby said, "on to the next one."

"We're going to cut more?" Lu asked.

"Damn right," Bobby said, swinging Clyde back up into the manure spreader. "We're going to block all the roads."

We shone our flashlights on the road behind us as Bobby backed up the way we had come. As we were coming back near the fork, we saw headlights approaching, a car coming out of our property.

"A car!" Lu called, her voice sounding quick and high.

We could see by the light of our flashlights that it was a small low car, with at least four guys inside. They had guns. They peered out at us.

"Hunters," Tuck whispered.

Two cars couldn't possibly fit alongside each other on the road. The car backed up, too, along with us. At the fork, Bobby veered up the turn, stopping by the corncrib so the other car could pass. The driver gunned the motor and shot forward, heading straight for the fallen tree.

Instead of continuing on down the hill though, Bobby turned the tractor off and we stayed where we were.

"What are we *doing*?" Clyde asked.

"Hiding," Tuck whispered, crouching down slightly, though it was dark.

Our mother called back at us. "Quiet, you guys."

We listened. The car had stopped. We heard doors slamming and voices swearing. Bobby laughed under his breath. Then the car was backing up, the same way we had. We saw it appear through the trees, its red backlights on. It was getting closer and closer. It seemed that the driver planned to veer up the fork as we had.

"They're going to hit us," Lu announced.

Just then Bobby turned the tractor back on. At the sound of the engine and view of the lights, the other car stopped. We, all of us, stayed very still. What would they do to us? I pictured them climbing out with their guns.

We didn't move. We heard a voice—"What the fuck?"— and then the car veered around in the little space there was, finally jumping forward and speeding down the hill.

"Whew!'" Bobby said. He laughed for real this time, and Tuck and Clyde started giggling crazily.

We drove down the hill to the spot by the creek where the big rock was. The big rock hung over the road. In the summer ferns sprouted from it and rivulets of water trickled down its sides. In the winter sometimes there were dagger-sized icicles hanging from its edge. The creek was frozen over but we could still hear the sound of water running underneath.

Our mother and Bobby went to find a second tree along the side of the road. Tuck and I examined the big rock for icicles. As were looking, there were headlights again, a pickup this time coming back from town. It slowed down.

"Hey, there." We recognized the voice. It was our neighbor, Tom Winter, who owned the sheep farm.

Our mother and Bobby stepped over to him.

"What in God's name are you people up to?" Tom Winter asked.

"Cutting down some trees," Bobby said, the chain saw in one hand.

"We're blocking the roads," our mother said.

"Keep the hunters out," Bobby said.

"How long is that going to keep a hunter out?" Tom Winter asked.

"Who knows? A day or so. It'll mess them up."

"They'll have to go back to their houses and get their chain saws," our mother said, sounding impish as she talked.

Tom Winter shook his head. He was missing half a finger from the clipping shears. "Don't know what you people got in your heads," he said somewhat gruffly, and drove on.

Bobby imitated him. "'Don't know what you people got in your heads.'" Our mother laughed.

She and Bobby stepped back over to the side of the road. I climbed up the rock and pulled off four icicles, handing them down one by one to Tuck. We distributed them among ourselves.

Bobby started cutting down the second tree. We stood back watching, sucking our icicles. The mixture was funny. They tasted like dirt and moss, but were clear and cold.

"We're going to get in trouble for this," Lu said to me softly so the boys wouldn't hear.

"With who?" I asked.

She shrugged nonchalantly, sucking her icicle. "Everyone: the bus drivers, the neighbors, the school."

I pictured how it would be the next day at school, arriving like renegades, keeping our heads down. We'd come by car. We'd have left one of the smaller roads open, so we could get out. But we'd have messed up the bus route. The bus would have had to turn around. It would arrive late, long after us, without all the kids. Would the teacher find out? Would she already know? A kid would ask, "How did you get here?" We'd shrug. We knew nothing.

So there would be things to worry about in the morning,

I saw what she meant, but for now I didn't care. The night air felt glassy, silver. After the second tree fell, Bobby started the tractor again. Two more trees to go. We clambered into the manure spreader. Our mother, standing beside Bobby, called back at us, "Everyone in?" Soon Bobby would be gone—our mother would ask him to leave—but for the moment she seemed happy. Only it was more than that. She, who rarely expressed any feeling clearly, seemed radiantly, even giddily, happy, to all of our surprise.

I MAY LOOK DUMB

On the weekends, our father picks us up in his funny-smelling car and takes us out into the world. "C'mon, c'mon, c'mon," he says, though we've been waiting for hours. He wears loose collarless shirts with embroidered fronts, bright red pants. He lives in the city now. We almost never go to his house. It isn't much of a place, on a little street in a not-so-good neighborhood, and there's nothing to do there. Rather, he always takes us on an adventure. Windows all down, hair flying, we peel out the driveway. The dust rises behind us on the dirt roads. The fields fall away. We're never sure what we're doing, where we're going, only that we're rapidly, recklessly, farmhouse by farmhouse, leaving all we know behind.

At the golf course, we turn. "Golf," our father says. "Now, who in his right mind would be so stupid to play golf?" We pass the neighbor Ed Trout's house, with the perfect garden. Every leaf and flower is in place and gleams. "You know what's going to happen to Ed Trout?" our father asks.

"What?!" Clyde, four now, screams.

"Jesus, Clyde, shut up." Lu, who's ten, covers her ear. He's screamed right into it.

"He's going to die and go up to Heaven, and at the gates where God is, God's going to ask him, 'What have you done?' And he's going to say, 'God, I've kept this perfect garden. It was perfect every day.' And God's going to shake his head, 'Sorry, Ed, that's not enough.' 'But I watered it every day.' 'Sorry, Ed.'"

By now we're looping up and down hills, soon to enter the little town. The funeral parlor is its stateliest building. There's the Vets Club, the post office, the elementary school. We stop at the gas station. We love the smell of gas. As soon as we pull in, we all start sniffing. Already some of us have to pee. We scramble out. There's a thin man with gray hair pumping the gas.

"Who wants an ice cream sandwich?" our father asks.

"Me!" we yell.

He goes into the office and gets ice cream sandwiches, one for each of us and two for himself. When we're back from the bathroom and our father's back from the office, we sit in the car unpeeling our ice cream sandwiches and waiting for the gas tank to be full.

"You know, it's the damnedest thing," our father tells us, gobbling his first sandwich in two bites. "Old guys just love it when you call them Pops."

"Really?" Lu asks. She licks her sandwich delicately, wrinkling her nose.

"Yes, they do. They do!"

The attendant comes over to our father's window, and our father hands him some cash.

"You mean like that guy?" Clyde asks.

"Well, I don't know about him. He's not that old. . . ."

Clyde leans his whole upper body out the window, his ice cream sandwich streaming down his hand, and screams, "Howdy, Pops!"

The guy, walking away, turns and shakes his fist at us.

Our father has already started the car and now pulls out fast. "Jesus, Clyde, not like that!" But he's hunched over, laughing. We're all laughing and hunched over now, too, like him, peering back at the guy as we make our getaway.

Our father hits on an enthusiasm and runs with it. Every weekend for months we go cave exploring. Then he switches. We go to tractor pulls or skiing or to meditate in ashrams. Sometimes he brings us places it takes hours to get to, like the top of a mountain, and then almost immediately he wants to leave. "C'mon, c'mon, c'mon," he says a thousand times over, herding us forward with his arms.

Occasionally he makes a scene. Once when we're walking down a street in Washington, D.C., he points out a group of punk rocker kids loitering near the park. They have high Mohawks, black and green, and wear spiked collars around their necks.

"You know what really drives these kids nuts?" our father says. "It really drives them nuts if you tell them they look nice. I'm going to go over there and tell them they look nice."

"No, Dad!" Lu says, stamping her foot.

But he's already on his way, head low, sidling slightly sideways. He looks back at us and wiggles his eyebrows up and down a few times.

We're standing on the sidewalk. Lu, desperate, turns away. I want to turn, too, but I can't make myself. I'm too curious. What are they going to do?

Our father edges up to the kids. The girl with the green hair deepens her sneer. The guy with the highest Mohawk leans back, looking our father up and down. Suddenly it occurs to me that they might attack him. Could they kill him? He's obviously provoking them. Might they not have knives?

Our father stands in front of them, wagging his finger, neck out like a turtle, telling them they look nice.

But instead of attacking him, they seem at a loss. They don't get it. Why's he doing this?

Having said his piece, our father turns away. But even then, it takes the kids a moment to recover. "Loser!" the one with the tallest Mohawk calls when he's already yards away. "Wanker!" the girl yells.

Our father looks back over his shoulder, nods and smiles at them, as if they've all just shared a little secret, and sidles his way back to us.

All of us are watching except for Clyde, who's kicking a tire on a nearby car. He kicks so hard his foot bounces back.

This is what makes it fun. Tuck's looking at our father, mystified. I feel like squirming. Lu's mad.

"Dad, why did you do that?!" she asks.

Both she and I want to get away fast.

Sometimes, because of his stutter, our father makes a scene without even meaning to. He gets stuck on a word and can't get it out. He stands there in front of whomever he's trying to talk to, mouth open, eyes closed, for the longest time. If we know what he's saying, we can help him out. The worst, though, is when he's on the phone. The people on the other end can't see his face, so have no idea what's going on. Sometimes they hang up or say something rude. We can't help either in that situation, so instead start giggling wildly.

"My kids are all laughing at me," our father tells the person on the line. For some reason, at this part, he doesn't stutter at all.

Whole blocks of our lives take place in the car. Our father talks a mile a minute, explaining things, telling us things, saying how his mind was "blown" by this or that. As he talks, we're supposed to tell him when he's hunching his shoulders—it's when he hunches that he stutters—

"Dad, you're pulling down," or when he's wrinkling his forehead, "You're wrinkling, Dad." He's concerned about the wrinkles on his forehead and about going bald. His hair is receding a bit in the front. He's all fired up about all kinds of things, a recent bill in Congress on education, an irrigation project, the lunatics and assholes all around us on the road. He loves it when we tease him. We tease him. We play games. We laugh so hard we pee. When someone farts, everyone yells and we roll all the windows down. Our father tells us that if you ever fart when there's a dog around, always act like it was the dog.

We scoot through a city, stopping at stoplights. The houses are all stacked on top of each other, the buildings full of little windows. Who lives here? The cracked sidewalks have grass sprouting up. We see two kids talking on the street down below. If a flood came, would all this be washed away? Then the light changes. We're out again, driving. We pass coal mines and dumping grounds with bulldozers lifting up and redepositing loads of trash.

"Keep your eyes out for cops," our father tells us. The cop cars wait stealthily in the center strip of grass. They usually pick a dip so they're out of sight. Sometimes our father gets stopped for speeding. One time he gets in a fight with the cop. He swears and bangs the top of the car with his hand.

"I'll see you in court," the cop says.

"Are you going to court?" I ask, once our father's back inside, thinking that means you go to jail.

He rants and raves about what an asshole the cop was and forgets about my question. It takes him a while to simmer down.

We get carsick, cranky. We beat on each other—no one wants to sit on the hump in the middle, someone in the backseat is taking all the room, whoever's in the front seat has been there too long. One of us cries or screams. Our father lets us go until it gets too bad. "All right, cut it out, you guys, Jesus Christ!" We fall silent, exhausted, and stare out the windows for hours and hours at the blue fog of New Jersey, the roadside developments, the thousands upon thousands of fleeting trees.

"Where are we going?"

"Are we almost there?"

Pit stops, pee stops. We love stopping and getting out of the car. If we're going north, our favorite place to eat is the Skyliner Diner. It's a silver metal building by the side of the road. We always order manicotti. One time, when we walk into the Skyliner, our father gets confused.

"Jesus Christ," he says, looking around, "what the hell's going on here? You've changed this whole place around!"

He's saying it to no one in particular, publicly. Clyde, standing beside him, does the same, imitating him, arms up, baffled, looking around. The cashier, a teenage girl with thin bangs and braces, is the only person working there in sight. She stares at our father blankly.

Our father tries again, edging nearer her. "Didn't you change this whole goddamned place around?"

She shakes her head slightly, then glances toward the back as if she might need help. It's not clear to her if he's crazy or not. Except for Clyde, who's stepped up to the cash register with our father, we're all lingering back.

"I swear to God," our father says, "they changed this whole place around." He turns and looks at us, one hand out, gesturing emphatically. "Didn't they? Didn't they?!"

The girl at the cash register still looks edgy. There's a little bell by her hand she can ring if she's in trouble.

Lu suddenly breaks away, walking past the cash register and down the aisle between the booths, her bright slab of hair swinging back and forth. A moment later, she turns and runs quickly back to us.

"It's because we came in the other door!" she says. "Usually we come in that door!"

"What?" our father says, full of disbelief. Or is he just playing? It's never quite clear if he's playing or not. He follows her back the way she went, with Clyde at his heels.

The cashier watches them go.

"Well, I'll be damned!" We hear our father laugh. Tuck and I follow the others across the diner. It does look more familiar on the other side.

"Damn," our father says, laughing, slapping his thigh. "She's right!" Clyde slaps his thigh, too, and laughs loudly like our father, only his laugh is fake, an imitation. "Good for you, Lu!" our father says. He loves when he's shown up to be a fool.

By the time we finish eating, it's dark. At night the road looks different, the red lights going away from us, the white lights coming toward us. Someone has to stay awake to keep our father awake. Lu and I pinch ourselves hard on the neck or inside of the thigh. Sometimes our father pulls over to sleep. He tilts the seat back. If you're wide-awake, you have to just sit there quietly. Or else he turns the radio on. This always helps because the love songs drive him crazy. *You came and you gave without taking. But I sent you away. Ohhhh, Mandy.*

"Jesus Christ, listen to this horseshit! Now, this is the kind of crock of shit only grown-ups would come up with."

"Grown-ups?" we say. "What's wrong with grown-ups?"

"What's *wrong* with grown-ups? What *isn't* wrong with grown-ups?" We're speeding through the night. We all lean up to listen, except Clyde who's asleep. We love it when our father rants and raves about grown-ups. "The real problem," he explains, "the overall problem, is that grown-ups think they're smarter than kids—when the fact of the matter is, the older you grow, the dumber you get. What happens is that you start hoarding up opinions. Pretty soon you've got an opinion stuck to everything, and before you know it, your poor little brain is so crowded with opinions the damned thing forgets how to think! Now, if grown-ups would only listen to their kids—if they'd listen to their kids—they might learn a thing or two." I laugh. Tuck grips his hands in his lap, excited. I can see Lu smiling to herself in the dark.

*

When our father brings a girlfriend along, things are different. She takes the front seat. The four of us in the back are crushed and quieter, waiting to see what she'll say. No matter what, we know we're in for a surprise.

Each of our father's girlfriends is weirder than the one before. There's Ginny, with a bowl haircut, who gets very nervous in the car. She keeps clutching the dashboard and the emergency brake. Whenever we stop, she gets out and walks off to the edge of the parking lot to try to calm herself down. Marcia puts a tape of people chanting mantras in the tape deck. Once when we go to a modern dance performance with her, instead of clapping along with everyone else, she lifts her arms up high in the air and twists her hands silently back and forth. Suzanne is a miniature person, so tiny you feel that she could fit into a box.

Although our father's girlfriends are very different from one another, not one of them, in any case, is at all like our mother, which turns them into a group. The unspoken line when we meet them is that our mother is the woman our father still loves, even though she told him to leave, and they, the girlfriends, are nothing more than stand-ins. We prefer it, of course, when our father comes on his own, but if a girlfriend's there, we're always curious. It's like an experiment in our science class: You put something in a petri dish, then nudge it, add water, waiting to see what it'll do.

For instance, our enthusiasm is sparked again by Ginny when we discover that she can't spell. We realize this one night in a hotel room when we sit down to play Boggle. Even Clyde can spell a few things. But when she comes up with a list of the most childishly misspelled words, we can't believe our eyes. At first we just stare at her. We hadn't realized that such a thing could happen to a grown-up. Then, without laughing, we're merciless. We very politely correct each word. Whenever possible, we take a special delight in letting Clyde do it. From then on, we insist on playing Boggle at every opportunity, over lunch, in the car. Even if she refuses, it's enough of a pleasure simply to be playing in front of her.

One day our father brings a woman named Abigail. She's the weirdest of all. She has her jaw wired shut due to an operation to get a bigger chin. This means she can only speak through a clenched jaw and take in liquids.

What's our father thinking? With these girlfriends, it's as if he's trying to convince himself of the uselessness of

pursuing any woman but our mother and, with such pecu-
liar choices, he proves himself right over and over again.
Not that he isn't pretty weird himself. He is—he even tries
to be. In this way, his girlfriends are like expressions of his
own weirdness, in which he delights, but they never seem
to step beyond that role. Until Lonnie.

It's our spring break and our father's coming to take us
to our grandmother's in New England. This is where we go
to ski in the winter and, when it's warmer, we sail or swim.
We'd thought our father was coming on his own, but when
he drives in, we see, to our annoyance, that there's a
woman in the car. From our perches, on the porch railing,
at the edge of the driveway, up above on the swing, we're
all ready to attack her, however silently, but then stop.
She's the kind of woman we've only seen in magazines or
on the rare occasions when we've watched TV—we don't
have a TV at our house—but never in real life. Stepping
out of the car and shaking out her perfumed hair, she looks
like an exotic bird that's just landed on our lawn. She wears
a see-through lime-green blouse that clings to her breasts, a
yellow skirt that stops above her knees. Her hair is long and
curly and dyed very blond, her eyelashes long and thick,
her lips glossed and shiny. This is a kind of glamour that

has nothing to do with the hippie style of our mother and her friends. Suddenly, we feel ashamed of the way we look, our straggly hair and corduroys. We feel ashamed of our yard, which is muddy from the rain. How is she supposed to get from the car to the porch in those high block heels?

She wobbles her way over, leans down and kisses us. She's brought presents, perfumes for my sister and me, shaving brushes for the boys. "For when you're old enough," she says in a playful voice. Tuck, his eyes on her, mesmerized, brushes the shaving brush back and forth across his chin. "And until then, you can use it to tickle girls." She laughs, winks at our father.

Only Clyde, it seems, is exempt—he's beating on the back of our father's leg with a stick, too much his own ball of energy to pay attention to anything else for long. But the rest of us are spellbound. No, she's definitely not "one of us." But is she maybe better instead of worse?

Once in the car, she promptly starts talking, in her light, flat, playful voice, like a girl's. Tuck, sitting on the hump in the middle, leans up close between the two seats and stares at her. She turns to kiss him. "This is my little man," she says. His cheeks are already bright red as always; now the edges of his ears flame too.

She looks back at Lu and me. "I've been dying to meet you," she says. "You know your father talks about you all the time. Ever since the first time we met. Did you tell them how we met?" she asks him. "Your father wooed me at a party, with his dancing. You know, he's a wonderful dancer. Do you girls like to dance? No one these days knows how to dance like that. Only aristocrats." She giggles. "So I knew right away he must be an aristocrat. An aristocrat in hiding, is what I thought. Because no aristocrat who wasn't hiding would wear such goofy clothes." She giggles again. "And I was right! Of course I was right! I'm always right about a man. So anyway, we danced. Everyone else was doing, you know, whatever funky dance, jiggling around, and then they put on a waltz and everyone got afraid except your father. I could see he wanted to dance. I was standing right there, looking at him. I don't know how to waltz either, but I figured I could learn." She hits our father lightly on the arm. "I figured there were a lot of things I could learn from an aristocrat."

"What's an aristocrat?" Tuck whispers to Lu.

Lu shrugs, putting up her hands. "Like kings and queens." She stares back at Lonnie, squinting, listening, trying to understand what she means.

I forget to peer out at the roadside houses, the rocks rising. I can't take my eyes off Lonnie. It's as if we've caught a butterfly in the petri dish and, rather than scrutinizing it, have become hypnotized. Most astonishing of all is that our father is mute. This is the first time we've seen this happen in our lives.

"When I went to Europe, I thought I was going to see aristocrats left and right," Lonnie goes on. "And, of course, I didn't see a single one! I told you about my trip to Europe, didn't I?" she says to our father, then turns back to us. "A man took me. He was very in love with me. But I said I'd only go if he didn't lay a finger on me." She giggles and holds out one dainty finger. "And he didn't. He didn't the whole time. I knew he wouldn't."

Then it occurs. Right in the middle of Lonnie's chatter, someone farts. We can't believe it. Mortified, we don't say anything at first. Lu very subtly rolls her window down. Only Clyde has no clue and acts the same as if it were any old day.

"Dad!" he yells.

"What?" our father asks.

I quickly hit Clyde on the leg, but it's too late.

"You farted!" Clyde yells, grabbing his leg.

"What?" our father asks, in his mock innocent voice. "Have I ever farted?"

Lonnie laughs her girlish laugh. "That's another thing I've learned. Only aristocrats fart like that."

"Damn!" our father says, leaning his head back. It's the look he gets when one of us has done or said something he finds wonderful. He couldn't be more pleased.

Last year, before it got too cold, we had been going with our father to leap off quarry cliffs. Our father's found out about a quarry that's right off the route to our grandmother's and wants to take us there.

"You got your suits, right?" he asks us, as he veers off the main road. Yes, we've brought our bathing suits. He nudges Lonnie, "You? You got your suit?"

"Oh, I couldn't," Lonnie says. "Jump off a cliff? I'd be much too scared. But I'll watch all of you."

Now we don't want to go, either. It means walking through the woods. How will she ever manage in her sandals? Her legs will get scratched. Burrs and leaves will stick in her hair. Suddenly, this quarry-jumping seems a dirty and boring pursuit.

But our father insists. We're going down side roads, our father ducking and peering to see if he's found the spot.

Finally, we stop in front of something that looks like a path. Our father parks the car and gets out. "C'mon, c'mon, c'mon," he says, since we seem to be lingering.

We trudge back along the bramble-lined path. I see Lonnie up ahead, picking aside the brambles gingerly with her fingers.

"Why do we have to do this?" I ask.

Our father, right in front of me, turns and looks back, truly surprised. I'm the one who's usually up for anything. "What d'you mean, why do we have to do this? Jesus Christ, I thought this was all you wanted to do!"

In some of the quarries, the water is crystal clear, but this time it's muddy. Great. We're going to plunge into muddy water right before Lonnie's eyes. We climb the cliff grudgingly. She waits below, a lime-green and yellow figure by the side of the water. I'm the first to leap. When I'm in the air, I hear Lonnie scream. Then when I come up again, my head bobbing on the surface of the water, she jumps up and down and claps her hands. "Whoo-ee!" she calls. She leans down to greet me as I swim over. "That was fantastic!" she says. Okay, I think, so maybe this isn't so bad. I pull myself out of the water. It's freezing, March, my skin is all blue. But this is definitely worth it all the same. If

Lonnie will clap and scream and jump up and down. The others leap behind me. Lonnie does the same for them. They beam, too, as they climb out of the water and then we all swagger as best we can midst our shivering up the cliff to do it again.

Afterward, we stop at a gas station. We're wet and bedraggled, but Lonnie looks splendid. When she steps out of the car, all the men look at her. Lu brings a comb with her into the bathroom to try to fix her hair. She usually wouldn't bother, but it's because Lonnie's there.

"Here," Lonnie says, "can I help you do that? You have the prettiest hair, you two. So thick." She begins combing out Lu's hair, and fixes the part. "Your father's just wonderful to me," she says as she works. "I only tell him these stories about other men to make him jealous." She turns on the hand dryer and makes Lu stand in front of it to dry her hair. Next she turns to me. Her perfume, when she's this near, is rising off her skin. Whereas I always tear at my hair, she's very gentle. Once it's all combed out straight, she turns on another dryer and has me stand there.

Then she looks at herself in the mirror, her face and hair. She opens her purse and takes out a makeup bag. Lu and I watch as she touches herself up, putting a layer or two more of mascara, pats of powder and lip gloss. "Hey!" she says, turning. "Do you two want me to make you up?" Usually it's a race between us and the boys to see who's done first in the bathroom. Now we're taking so long, but we don't care. Lu and I nod. Lu steps up first. Lonnie makes her close her eyes. She puts eye shadow on Lu's lids and curls her lashes. "You don't want mascara," she says, "mascara's messy." She dabs lip gloss on Lu's lips and a touch of blush on her cheeks. "There!" she says, stepping back and looking. She steps near again, wetting a finger in her mouth and shaping Lu's eyebrows. My hair is now dry too. Lonnie runs her hands through it. She shivers. "Oh, it's like silk," she says. She puts makeup on me too. I love the feeling, eyes closed, of her cool, smooth hands running over my face.

Our father knocks on the bathroom door. "What's the holdup?"

"It's a surprise, you'll see," Lonnie says.

"Jesus!" we hear him say, turning away. We giggle. We know how he hates just hanging around.

When we come out, our father's back in the car with the boys. Both Lu and I have eye shadow on and very pink cheeks.

"Look at them," Lonnie says. "Did you ever see such pretty girls?"

Lu, with her makeup on, has an uncertain smile.

"What do you have on?" Clyde asks. He swipes at Lu's face.

Tuck looks at us for a minute then goes back to staring at Lonnie. "This one doesn't need makeup," Lonnie says, rubbing Tuck's chubby cheeks and kissing him.

Our father snorts a little. Besides having been made to wait around, this—makeup and so on—is not at all his line.

*

Usually with our father we stay in a cheap hotel. Or we just drive straight the whole way through, him stopping to lie back for naps now and then. But this time, he's made arrangements to spend the night with a friend of his in Boston. We twist and turn our way through Boston until we find the street, quiet, clean, lined with large trees. The house is a brownstone, the door painted a shiny dark blue. Our father holds Clyde up so he can bang the knocker. He bangs it loud.

The man who appears, our father's friend, George, looks much older than our father though they're the same age. Amazingly tall, with a protruding belly, he already looks like an old man.

"Good Lord," he says to our father, "what a wondrous shirt." As he says hello to Lonnie, a slight smile plays at the corners of his lips. He gives the four of us perfunctory nods, then leads us all into the house.

The house is dark inside and, though it's the height of spring, it feels like winter here, the windows small and lots of dark furniture all around. A woman, who must be a maid—though we've never seen a maid, but she wears a black-and-white costume—peers out of a door.

"Do you need anything?" she asks.

"No, no, that's fine," George says, "We'll eat when Pat returns. Pat's out teaching a class," he says over his shoulder, leading us down a dark hallway.

"She's teaching, is she?" our father asks. "A professor, you said? Damn! Good for her."

George sounds surprised. "Well, yes, I suppose so."

We follow him down the hall to a room where there's a TV on. Two kids are there. They look up.

"Say hello, boys," George says.

The boys, his sons, look just tiny, given their father's massive size, and seem to be sitting on miniature doll chairs. Or at least one of them does. The other is handi-capped and in a wheelchair. He's very frail. His arms and legs wobble. The first one, short, pale and chubby, sits very near to take care of his brother.

At first we feel offended by being brought in here. When he's ranting about grown-ups, our father goes on and on about how stupid people are not to want kids around.

"And," we ask, egging him on, "what about parties where there are no kids allowed?"

"No kids allowed?! Who would want to go to a party where there were no kids allowed?"

These children, it seems, are always shut up in here.

But we stop thinking about it a moment later because we're watching TV. Since we never watch TV, we don't know how to do it. I look at Tuck. He hasn't even sat down but his eyes are already spinning. Clyde sits openmouthed, very close to the screen, his legs tucked underneath him. Lu and I are soon doing the same. We forget about everything, the boys, the house, even our father and Lonnie. We don't know how much time has passed when the maid comes to get us. The maid pushes the boy in the wheelchair into the dining room and the rest of us follow behind.

The dining room is dark, with a dark wood oiled table and a sideboard. George's wife, Pat, is there. She has dark hair, slim legs, and an ironic expression that never seems to go away. She, like the rest of the family, wears somber clothes, burgundy and dark blue. We all look completely out of place, our father in his hippie clothes, Lonnie in her transparent lime green blouse, Lu and I in velour V-necks, Tuck with the Indian belt he wove himself holding up his corduroys. The boy in the wheelchair is placed at one end and the rest of us kids around him.

The maid brings out the food, a meat-and-potato stew in a deep dish. Lonnie, as usual, immediately starts talking. "Are you really a professor?" she asks Pat.

"I am," the woman says, smiling her ironic smile.

"I think that's wonderful," Lonnie says. "So romantic."

Pat's laugh sounds like a bark. "Well, I don't know about that. What do you do?" Pat asks. She has a throaty voice. She doesn't look at Lonnie as she's asking because she's serving herself food.

Lonnie clasps her hands and props her chin on them. "Oh, nothing," she says. "Loll around."

Pat looks at her, raising one dark eyebrow.

"That's not true," our father says, pointing at Lonnie. "She's a psy-psy-psychologist. And not just any kind of psychologist. She works in a mental hospital."

This is news to us. We all look at Lonnie. I picture her in a hospital hallway wearing a nurse's uniform, with those white shoes. She must look very pretty, I decide. I picture the part around her boobs very tight.

"Did you have to tell them that?" Lonnie says playfully, looking down at her hands. "Well, anyway, that's just my day job." She flutters her eyelids and laughs. Suddenly, as opposed to Pat, she seems to have the most charming giggly laugh.

Our father persists, still pointing at Lonnie. He must be nervous because he's stuttering. "She p-p-put herself through college all on her own—"

"Oh, come on, let's not talk about that," Lonnie says. "I want to talk about other things, romantic things, art and literature. That's what we came here for. Isn't that what you all usually talk about?"

There's a beat of awkward silence. Lonnie looks around, dazzled, then down at her plate. "These plates are so pretty!" she says. "Are they new?"

"No, no, dear," George says, that same amused expression on his face he had when he first saw her, "those plates are very old."

Lonnie blushes. "Oh, well, of course, listen to how gauche I am. They're very pretty anyway. I guess the oldest things are the prettiest, like those paintings. I guess those paintings are very old too."

"Why, yes, dear, they are."

Lonnie puts on her flirty eyes. "Do you call all women 'dear,' or only the ones who ask silly questions?"

"No, not at all, your questions are most perspicacious," George says. He leans back, folding his long-fingered hands on his chest, and smiles. He seems to be enjoying this.

"See now, there's a word I don't know," Lonnie says. "I knew I'd learn things if I met some of Sam's friends. I asked him, I said, on this trip I want to meet some of your friends, not your new friends—he's got the weirdest friends now—but your old friends from the past. But he keeps you all in hiding, I don't know why. If I had such nice friends, I'm sure I'd introduce them to everyone. I'd bring whole troops of people in here."

George, listening for a moment, then turns to our father

and addresses him, interrupting. "You sure ducked out of sight," he says. "What have you been up to?"

Lonnie looks very surprised. Although the rest of us are still listening to her, she lets her story peter out.

"Aww, all kinds of things," our father says. He's acting different, not like himself. "Writin' a bit, got some other projects, started up a little business."

"Oh, really? What kind of business?"

"Chimneys. I'm a chimney man."

"Chimneys? Good Lord, you're just as bullocks as ever! Have you kept up with any of our partners in crime at the AD?"

"Naww, not so much."

"C'mon, fella, where's your allegiance? A group of us get together once a month."

"Oh, yeah, who do you see?"

Lonnie leans across the table toward us and asks in a loud whisper, "What's the AD?"

Lu shrugs, lifts her hands. "Dad, what's the AD?" she interrupts.

George looks confused by such impertinence from a child. Pat is watching all of us, amused, as if we were a circus act.

"Aww, it's a club at Harvard," our father says.

"What's Harvard?" I ask. Lonnie laughs delightedly.

"It's a school where George and I went."

George has a kind of harrumphing laugh. "Well, you've certainly been keeping them in the dark," he says.

"Oh, yes," Lonnie says, "he's been keeping us all in the dark. About everything. Believe me, he's got things up his sleeve. And I don't mean just you two. I mean all sorts of projects, not to mention women. And here I am an open book. I guess all aristocrats are secretive, aren't they?" She turns to Pat, pointing at George. "Is he secretive too? I tell everything. He knows about all the men I've dated and slept with. I've told him all the stories. I try to make him jealous, but he doesn't get jealous. Isn't that the weirdest thing?" Again turning to Pat and pointing at George: "Does he get jealous? Maybe that's another trait—"

"Charming, you're charming, dear," George interjects, as if trying to put some order into the proceedings. "Yes, we're all very secretive, aren't we? I, for example, hardly ever enumerate to my wife the women I slept with before I met her. Or perhaps I did once. Did I once, darling?"

"Yes, dear, once," Pat says, "in Cairo, right before the war."

"Cairo? Before the war?" Lonnie looks confused. There's a tremor on her lips, though she keeps her smile. "You're making fun of me, aren't you?"

"No, dear, not at all," George says.

"Why do you seem to have a British accent?" Lonnie asks. "Are you British? Or is it just a little playacting? We all do a little playacting, don't we, even aristocrats, to get by?"

George, annoyed, scrapes back his chair. "I think we've finished here, haven't we?" He calls the maid. "We'll have coffee in the living room."

Everyone stands. Lonnie's comment was a barb, but now she looks sorry. George is already lighting up a cigar. He doesn't look at her. There's a move toward the living room, George first. The chubby son pushes the one in the wheelchair out past the living room and down the hall again to where the TV room is. Clyde follows them. But Lu, Tuck, and I linger in the hall, not sure where we're supposed to go. Our father, George, and Pat are already sitting down in the living room. Lonnie has gone to the bathroom. When she reappears coming down the hall, she says to us in a whisper, "Let's go watch TV, okay?"

She pauses in the door of the living room. "I'm going to go watch TV with them," she says. "I'll let you aristocrats talk amongst yourselves."

George looks relieved, but our father seems disappointed. He holds out a hand to Lonnie. "Honey," he says, to our surprise. We've never heard him call a woman "honey" before. But Lonnie's decision has been made.

We bring her into the TV room with us. We sit down on the couch with her, Lu and me on one side, Tuck on the other. We hand her the flicker so she can choose a good channel. We find her a blanket for her bare knees. "Oh, whew," she says, still blushing, recovering, "this is so much more fun in here with you."

✳

The next day begins as the previous one, only something seems to have shifted in the night. Who decides it? Me? Lu? We have to get rid of Lonnie, or depose her at least. She requires too much attention. She's disrupted everything. Our father has been silenced, he calls her "honey"; we're all now decorous. Gone are the games, the farts, the hair-flying fun. The night before at dinner we saw her weak spot. This gives us a grip. We're no longer helpless, blindly enthralled.

Once again, in the car, Lonnie begins chattering right away. "Spanish men are just wonderful. Have you ever dated a Spanish man? Well, I guess, of course, you haven't. Though your father might have, knowing him." She giggles. "Your father's a complete schizophrenic, you know that, right? But that's what I seem to like: crazy people. At least they're always full of surprises. Your father is definitely always full of surprises. And that's what a woman wants, isn't it, to be surprised? It's the biggest aphrodisiac."

"What's an aphrodisiac?" Lu asks, but differently now, warily.

"Oh, they don't need to know this yet, do they?" Lonnie says. "It's what your father has. It's what brings the girls around. Everyone's in love with your father. Wherever we go, all the girls are wild for him."

I give a little snort, picking up on our father's snort yesterday over the makeup.

Tuck sits slowly back. Lu sighs, looking out the window. Lonnie must have felt us all pulling away, but chatters valiantly on.

"I think the Italians are way overrated. That's just a movie myth. The ones I've met all look like worms."

She takes out some lip gloss and puts it on, then hands it back to Lu and me.

"No, thanks," Lu says, her hand flopping down casually, staring back out the window again. I'm torn. I remember how the lip gloss felt on my lips the day before and how it had the nicest strawberry taste. "No, thanks," I say, my voice a bit weak.

"Are you sure?" Lonnie asks.

I nod, somewhat pained.

"It stinks in here," Clyde says after a moment.

We all look at him. We don't smell anything.

"Did someone fart?" Tuck asks. We're not even worried now about talking about farts in front of Lonnie, whereas yesterday we were so concerned.

"No, it's not a fart," Clyde says, laughing, slapping his knee. "It smells like something else. Even stinkier."

"Perfume," Lu and I murmur softly in unison.

Lonnie turns around in her seat and gives us a quick stung look, then addresses Clyde. "You don't like my perfume?" There's a tremor on her lips, that same tremor that was there the night before, only she kept trying to smile. Everyone sees it except for Clyde. He's not even looking.

"No, I don't!" he says, laughing.

"All right, Clyde," our father says. "That's enough."

We drive on for a little while. Lonnie actually isn't talking. When she starts again, her voice sounds different. Not so much like a little girl's. "You know, I didn't have a childhood like you all do. You're very lucky. You have two parents who love you. You don't have to work all the time. You're free to play. We lived in a trailer. My father abandoned us. I worked nonstop. I almost never had any fun."

Our father looks over at her, uneasily.

She tries to rally one last time, in her girlie voice again, giving our father eyes. "That's why I've made up for it as an adult."

Our father laughs with relief, but we, by this point, are all looking away.

A little while later, in the gas station bathroom, in what seems like a last-ditch effort, Lonnie tells Lu and me that she's so in love. Our father, she says, is the love of her life. Lu, without looking at her, shakes the water off her hands. I eye Lonnie warily. I went into one of the stalls after her.

"Did you write that on the wall?" I ask.

She giggles. On the wall in the bathroom were the words *Lonnie will marry Sam this year* in lipstick. Lu goes into the stall to look, too, and comes back out and stares at Lonnie. Lonnie blushes.

"Yes, I did."

"Why?" I ask, on my lip a slight sneer.

"Why? Because I wanted to. Didn't you ever like a boy and write his name on a wall?"

"No," both Lu and I answer.

"Well, you should."

"Why?" I ask.

"We don't want to," Lu says.

We can tell from the look on Lonnie's face that she sees that everything has changed. She turns to the mirror and fixes her makeup silently. Lu and I head for the door.

Later, it occurs to me that Lonnie illustrated perfectly one of our father's favorite lines: "I may look dumb." He loved the idea of someone "looking dumb." Her Barbie doll act was just that, an act, the way she'd come up with of getting by.

Back in the car again, we drive on. Lonnie is quiet. Sensing something wrong, our father jokes around a bit. But he seems to be waiting for Lonnie to talk and can't get his usual monologue off the ground. After a little while, Lonnie asks if we can stop again, saying she has to use the bathroom. Once our father pulls over, she steps out, taking her purse, and then, leaning down at the window, asks for the keys. Our father hands her the keys. She goes around and opens the trunk, takes out her bag, baby pink, and comes back around.

"Thanks," she says, leaning down, dropping the keys on the passenger seat. "I'm going. Your kids, you know, are mean."

We're all struck silent as she walks off. Only then does our father make a move. "Jesus Christ," he says, getting out of the car and following her into the office. We can see the two of them through the glass window. Lonnie has asked the guys behind the counter to use the phone and is making a call when our father comes in. He waits for her to finish. When she puts the receiver down, he begins gesturing, pointing back to the car. She shakes her head, her long yellow curls flopping around. He moves toward her. She steps back. He throws his arms up in the air, in a helpless gesture. The guys behind the counter are watching with the animated faces of spectators fully engrossed in the show. Lonnie starts talking forcefully, pointing a finger at our father. Then she's yelling. He puts his hands up in front of his face, as if he's being hit by hail. A blue cab pulls up in front of the office. Lonnie picks up her bag and steps out. Our father dodges gingerly after her. Outside, she gets in the cab and slams the door. He taps on the window. She doesn't look. A few seconds later, the cab drives off. She doesn't look back at any of us.

Our father stands outside the office, looking after the cab. Then he looks over at us and raises his hands again, helpless, in the air. He slinks back to the car. "Damn!" he says, getting in. We kids are all a bit excited. This is surely exciting. Of course it would have been more so had Lonnie screamed more. And if it had gone on. If she hadn't driven off like that without looking back. We giggle nervously. But much too soon, the blue cab is out of sight.

Our father leans back for a moment, hands in his lap, staring out the windshield. We almost never see him like this, not talking or moving. Then he starts the car. Lu climbs through the space between the seats into the front. We drive out of the gas station, drive on. Silence. No one talks. Isn't this what we'd wanted? The situation was impossible. There was no question. She had to go. I glance around, but no one is looking at one another. Are we ecstatic, triumphant? Do we feel that we've done a terrible thing? Have we even done anything at all? I lean up to look at our father's face. He's staring out impassively at the road. I settle back and stare out too. We're on the highway. The landscape looks lonely, the cliffs and road signs, the wayside houses.

As we drive on, I keep noticing for some reason the deposits of roadside trash, tumbling down the hills beyond the guardrails. You can see the way the stuffed armchairs, the bedsprings, and the toilet bowls have dropped and, by their own weight, bumped down the hill. I know that Lonnie went off of her own accord, yet I can't help feeling at the same time that we dumped her. That we rolled her out of the front seat and dumped her by the roadside. Sitting there, I can almost feel it, the strain in my arms, from heaving a body out of the car.

INTERVENTION

Whenever they went to their grandparents in New England, it felt like they were coming from an island to the world, though it was a funny sort of version of the world. The all-night drive along highways with their father, making pit stops, and then as they were waking, coming to the little town, pristine, with a white-steepled church. They'd pass through the town, cross the humped bridge, take a left and glide along past roadside houses until they came to two stone pillars where they turned again. The house couldn't be seen from here, but bit by bit as they approached, parts of it appeared, the four wide chimneys, the front room windows, others blotted out by trees, until, as they veered in the circular drive, too soon, it was upon them.

*

Maeve walked out around the circular drive, the dog, Milton, half German shepherd, half greyhound, loping behind her. She crossed the drive, took a turn and then saw it, her grandmother's garden. But could that really be called a garden? It looked more like a jungle. Each year Maeve went to look and each year the garden had grown wilder. Instead of weeding, her grandmother kept planting. The asparagus plants sprayed out their feathery limbs, tall as trees. There was a whole field of sunflowers—they were new—as was the crawling squash plant, down-covered, long-leaved, threatening to strangle the green-pepper plants. The compost heap rose like a black mountain. The tomato plants hung drunkenly from their sticks. Maeve circled the fence until she found the gate, lifted the hook and stepped inside.

She picked her way through, here squishing a tomato, there getting pricked by a weed with needles. It had rained the night before. Now and then, off a leaf, a drop still fell. In the dark under one of the squash leaves, she saw something glowing. She stepped nearer, held her breath. It was a flower, ghostly pale purple with a deep throat. It set off in the dark of its recess an exhilarating, unsettling gleam.

*

Lu peered down from the attic window. It was a dizzying height. She saw Maeve's head disappearing around the circular drive, and then: no one. The yard was empty. In the distance, she could see the humped back of the mountain, covered with pines. She turned and listened below. Nothing. She crept back to the closet she had been looking through. There were many of them. The attic, like the rest of the house, was huge. There was a broad hall that you entered when you climbed the attic stairs, then three large rooms, once the bedrooms of the growing children—this was where they moved to get away from the parents—and then of their friends, and then of whoever else settled here, a small back room, a bathroom, and an enormous dark expanse known as the storage attic. But the rooms were hardly visible as such. They were, all of them, crammed with things, trunks full of relics, stacks of mattresses, oriental screens, piles upon piles of broken chairs. There were valuable objects, like paintings, tucked away between moth-eaten lampshades. But it was not only the attic that was like this. Everywhere, in this house, things were hoarded.

It was here among the closets stuffed with old clothes,

from her aunt's time, her grandmother's, and sometimes even further back than that, that Lu, now eleven, made her discoveries. Every time she came here, she found wondrous things—a hatbox lined with silk, a velvet cape, purple high-heeled shoes. Sometimes when you touched a dress, it disintegrated entirely. She'd go back home again, something new and wondrous stuffed in her bag. Now from a pile of shoes on one of the closet floors she pulled out a rabbit fur boa. She draped it over her shoulders. She pulled it close around her neck. She craned to look in the mirror on top of an old dresser. The mirror had silver spots on it. You had to position yourself just right in order to see anything. The boa illuminated her face, illuminated her dirty-blond hair. It was a trick, an invention. Dust, as she stood there, jubilant, crept across the floor.

*

Tuck, seven, peered into his grandfather's study. What was he doing in there now? There was a narrow tunnel between the high shelves of papers and books. In the back was a workshop. Tuck had never been inside. But he knew enough to be desperately curious. He pictured steaming bottles and a tank with layers of ice. Because hadn't his grandfather been inventing a way to make snow? He was building a ski lift up the humped back of the mountain, but first he'd had to invent a way to make snow. Only then it seemed someone else had invented it first. Tuck also knew about the other things: the sailboat his grandfather was building, the fastest in the world, the hay drying machine, the speedometer to put on your skis, so you'd know how fast you were going. (But then how could you read it if you were going that fast?) Tuck would never dare go into his grandfather's study. He would never even knock. He would just wait like this, breathing, near the door.

*

But the place in that house was the kitchen. The walls were eggshell blue, the ceiling papered with silver wallpaper. The cord of the lamp above the kitchen table was wrapped up in a wooden cooking spoon because otherwise it fell too low. The table was always piled with food: Swiss rye crackers, oatcakes, maple syrup, cherries and dried apricots and a funny type of fig, cold cooked rice, brewer's yeast, hot pepper sauce, steamed kale, someone's recent lunch of caviar and rum. The refrigerator was packed to the brim. But despite this weight of accumulation, the room was airy.

The door leading out to the backyard, also eggshell blue, was invariably left open. Light came through the windows on either side of the stove, outlining avocado plants in various states of growth, illuminating an old flour grinder screwed to the counter, and the dishes piled pell-mell in the sink. Everyone sooner or later gravitated here.

"I came in here—we came in here—this morning," their father, Sam, said, his voice sounding funny because Clyde, up in his arms, was holding his nose closed, "and there was some guy, never seen him in my life, cooking himself an omelet." He pulled his nose away. "Now, who the hell was that?"

"Was it Reb?" Clyde's uncle Lewis asked. He was leaning against the sink eating an apple. The youngest of the five siblings, he still lived in this house. He had a large handsome bony head, with a long ponytail down his back.

"I don't know what the hell the guy's name was. He acted like *I* was interrupting *him*."

"Well, he probably didn't know who you were," Lewis said. "Maybe it was Crow."

"Who the hell's Crow?"

Lonnie, Sam's girlfriend, sitting at the table, giggled. She was wearing a tight pink sweatsuit and horn-rimmed glasses and was flipping through a magazine called *Psychology Expert*.

"Crow's working on the tenant houses. They need all kinds of repairs. And Reb, well, Reb's one of Coralie's finds. But he's helping Dad out with an engineering project."

"An *engineering* project? *That* guy's helping Dad with an *engineering* project?" Sam said.

"Well, yes, apparently. He's supposed to be brilliant."

"*Brilliant? That* guy?"

Clyde's grandmother, Rita, hovering around the stove, smiled slightly in Sam's vicinity without looking at him directly. She had a delicate figure, dark shiny hair cut in a bob, an almost large nose. She wore her garden clothes, a lavender blouse, a blue jean skirt, and sandals.

Lonnie looked up. "It says here that dangling earrings scare sixty percent of men away." Just then, Lu drifted in from the hallway, pulling a strand of hair out of her mouth. Lonnie raised a finger and looked right at her. "Never wear dangling earrings on a first date."

Lu's response was faint, noncommittal. She drifted over to the almond jar. She couldn't believe their father had brought Lonnie here.

"So what's this engineering project?" Sam asked Lewis,

jerking his head toward the hallway and the grandfather's study door.

"It's an alternative energy contraption, the idea being to exploit the temperature differences in a given water body. Truth is, I haven't got it entirely straight. But Dad's thinking big, like harnessing the ocean."

"Damn! All right," Sam said.

Rita spoke softly, maybe even impishly, or was it despair? "About a month ago, I came around the side of the house and he was there with a man discussing the foundation stones."

"What do you mean, 'the foundation stones'?" Sam asked.

"Oh, you know, those beautiful big stones that hold up the house. Well, they were discussing the price of those stones." Rita put a strangely textured pancake on a plate and moved to sit down at the kitchen table.

"Oh . . ." Lonnie laughed, covering her mouth. This was her first visit to the house.

Sam, excited, put Clyde down. "Jesus Christ, Mum, so the goddamned guy is really losing his mind."

Rita shrugged, looked away vaguely. "The appraiser's

coming tomorrow. He thinks we can get a good price for the American bladderback chairs."

Christopher, the other uncle, dressed impeccably in a white shirt and black pants, entered through the back door, holding a tight ball of clothes in his arms. "Oh, oh, oh, what's all this?" he said, looking through his thick glasses, clearly appalled to see them all. "Upp, upp, hello, Sam, hello" (to Lonnie). He headed, without stopping, straight for the pantry where the washing machine was. Lu looked at him. She remembered how they all said he was the smartest one, with "a mind like a steel trap." She thought of that steel trap inside his head, clamping down on an animal's neck. He lived not in the house but in a filthy shack out in the woods. All the same, his clothes were always impeccable.

Sam bowed somewhat mockingly as Christopher passed and went into the pantry.

"Is that Christopher?" Lonnie asked Sam in a stage whisper, once the pantry door was closed.

Sam nodded.

Lu dropped three more almonds into her mouth from a height. Clyde held out his hand for some.

Christopher reappeared.

"How's the fish biz?" Sam asked him.

"Good, good," Christopher answered, already making a beeline back out of the kitchen.

Lonnie turned in her chair as Christopher passed. "I've heard the most wonderful things about you," she said. "Like that you can play chess blindfolded and that you never lose."

Christopher laughed abruptly, mirthlessly. "Oh, oh, well, I've been known to do that, yes."

"They say you do it in the bars in town and you win every time. Oh"—Lonnie said, giving an excited jump like a little girl—"I want to see!"

Christopher laughed with a bit more pleasure. "Well, perhaps another time." He turned in tight circles, like an animal in a corral, trying to get out. "No, no, can't stay. Got lots to do."

He left like a shot, closing the door closely behind him.

"The pumpkin squash I planted has the most extra-ordinary flower," Rita said, "the palest purple you've ever seen."

✳

There was the eggshell-blue kitchen, its paint peeling in all the corners, the stretch of dark hall and then at the end the magical lamp, attached to the wall. Magical how? If you tapped it once, on its copper neck, it lit up very dimly, if you tapped it again, it grew brighter and again, brighter still. Then, to turn it off, you simply tapped it down again, tap, tap, tap, gently, and it sank bright to dim to dimmer until it was fully out. Lu, having trailed out of the kitchen again and down the hall, reached up, kept tapping.

*

Clyde knew there was a stuffed wolf somewhere. Everyone said so. He'd checked the attic last time. Now he'd look in the basement. The door to the basement was off the kitchen. Maybe the wolf was there. Clyde sneaked down the set of dark stairs.

In the basement, lightbulbs hung from the ceiling on strings. Leaning up along one wall were skis, fifty, sixty pairs at least, battered, some broken, worn by generations. Then, beside them, in the shadows, ski poles, a whole pile of wooden poles. And boxes and boxes of ski boots, the leather kind, cracked, and skates, both hockey skates and figure skates, some missing blades. The skates and boots spilled out onto the floor. But nobody, no matter what, threw anything away. On the contrary, they collected.

There was never just one of anything. Instead there were always twenty, fifty, hundreds. (In the kitchen, it was the same: there were thirty eggbeaters, fifteen colanders, an enormous collection of plastic yogurt containers.) No one was thinking of utility here. In the basement, there were also collections of magazines, hundreds upon hundreds of magazines heaped in stacks in long rows, architecture magazines, *Time* and *Life, National Geographic.* There was even a smaller collection of *Playboy*s. With the hanging bare bulbs overhead, the light was either dim or glaring. Clyde crossed a glaring patch of floor over to the other side, where the shelves were.

The shelves were maybe even the most interesting part, Clyde thought. One was lined with irons, of all shapes and sizes, from all different time periods, most of them rusty, standing on end or lying flat. Another shelf held toasters, every kind of toaster, it seemed, that had ever been invented. Then there were ear trumpets, again from the very small, the opening the size of a child's outstretched palm, to the enormous, elephant size—how could anyone hold it? There were chemistry sets, with all sorts of potions in small glass jars. The glass jars were dusty. Everything, everywhere, was covered with dust. As always, Clyde pictured finding something deliciously horrible between the dusty jars, like, he pictured, a faded old nose.

*

"It's a tufted titmouse," Rita said, looking out the kitchen window at the birdfeeder.

Tuck was beside her, preparing himself a grilled cheese sandwich in the toaster oven. He pulled himself up on the counter to see.

"Heyyy!" A scruffy-looking guy, lean with tanned arms, opened the kitchen door. He had overalls on, but he hadn't hooked the bib up so they were drooping, the shoulder straps trailing on the floor. "Oops, oops, 'scuse me, sir," he said to the dog, Milton, who had been waiting to go out. The young man danced delicately around the dog, held the door open for him, bowed, then, looking up, addressed everyone—"Hello, amigos!"—and crept like the Pink Panther, Tuck thought, across the kitchen to the other doorway, where he could be heard tapping on the grandfather's study door.

"That's him," Lonnie whispered, giggling to Sam. "The engineer." She was still flipping through her magazine at the table.

"Yeah, right. Jesus Christ," Sam said. He and Lewis were lifting the stove pipe out of the big woodstove. As they took it down, a rain of soot fell over their heads and shoulders.

Suddenly, out the kitchen window, all the birds flew up. A car had just pulled in and a woman had gotten out. Tuck, sitting up on the counter, recognized her through the window. She was Lewis's girlfriend, Coralie, and had been around for several years. A moment later, she barged through the kitchen door. Jaw set, eyebrows low, she seemed to be on a mission.

"Lewis," she said, "you won't believe what I just saw. I was just in Kmart and they're having a sale of the most incredible diamond earrings. They were stunning, really stunning. And cheap for what they are. I mean really cheap. Only a hundred and fifty dollars."

"Jesus Christ," Sam said softly. Lewis, covered with soot, winced.

Coralie turned and saw Lonnie in her sweatsuit. Her expression changed completely. "Wow, you were working out."

"Oh, no, I never work out. I just wear the clothes and hope I'll lose weight," Lonnie answered.

"Uh-huh. You just wear the clothes, right?" Coralie looked at Lonnie's magazine. "You're a psychologist, right?" she asked.

Lonnie winked. "That's my day job."

"Oh, wow, that's so funny. That's your day job," Coralie said.

"Here's thirty," Lewis said, handing Coralie some cash.

"Thirty?" Coralie's face changed. She looked disgusted all at once. "What am I going to do for thirty dollars?"

Up above, there was a clanging sound of beer bottles tumbling down the staircase and loud punk music suddenly began.

*

When they came in winter, the house was surrounded by snow. Ski tracks led from the front and back doors and then down the road and out across the fields. In the afternoon light, the tracks were full of blue shadows. The blue lines fanned out in diagonals. They opened up around the house like an unfolding fan. The tennis court was covered with snow. The scalloped birdbath was heaped with snow. Snow piled up on the curved branches of the pines. It covered the pond, unless they'd been skating and cleared it off.

But standing now under the copper beech tree alongside the tennis court, Lu couldn't believe that there had ever been snow. No, it seemed impossible, with everything so green. The pond was murky green in the shallows, darker in the middle. The grass was green and soft and full. Above her, the leaves of the copper beech tree, dark red, smelled like no other leaves. It was an easy tree to climb. The bark was gray and very smooth. It even had wrinkles, in the joints, like elephant skin, where a branch met the trunk. In the fall, the leaves were copper-gold. It was as if a huge torch had been lit up and was burning in the yard. The whole tree shone. Its gold light fell through the windows of the house, into the library and onto the waterbed in their grandmother's bedroom above.

❋

Lonnie was standing up now in the kitchen, her horn-rimmed glasses perched on her head. "Okay, I mean, so I get the picture that all these people live here. But, I mean, what do they *do*?"

She looked over at the teenage kid standing by the counter on the other side of the room, headphones on, making himself some tea. He was about sixteen, scrawny and white, and so thin he had to hold his pants up with one hand.

"For example," Lonnie asked, "who is he?"

Sam was now sweeping out the chimney of the stove, with Clyde beside him, handing him tools.

"He's May's son, our eldest sister, by an early marriage," Sam said.

"And May?"

"She's not around. Now she's married to a New York lawyer. He doesn't like coming here."

"I mean, the weird thing," Lonnie went on, "is that it's like they were hippies before there were even hippies, or back-to-the-landers, or whatever. I mean, right? What else do you call this kind of lifestyle? With the organic garden, the inventions, all these wacky people running around? And the pot, right, I mean, 'the engineer's' a total pothead, and I wouldn't be surprised if Lewis were too. I guess the difference is the money."

The teenager, Alex, suddenly piped up. "And the politics. The old boy's politics are completely futile. I wouldn't be surprised if he opposed the Emancipation Proclamation."

"Really?" Lonnie turned and looked at Sam.

Sam shrugged helplessly.

There was a thumping in the hall against the paneled walls. Clyde ran out to see what it was. "It's Maeve on the unicycle!" he said, running back to report, then turning and running back to look. There was more thumping and a crash.

Lonnie looked back at Alex, who had put his headphones back on and wasn't paying attention anymore. She turned again to Sam. "They started out with tons of money, right?"

"Yeah, yeah, sure," Sam said. He was covered with soot from head to toe. "Dad even had a houseman for his clothes."

"And now what?" Lonnie asked Sam. "Is there money being generated?"

"Are you kidding?" Sam said.

"Nothing? But that's crazy."

Sam shrugged again, helplessly.

Maeve appeared in the doorway on a unicycle, rode it into the kitchen, wobbled, caught her balance, turned around.

❋

Clyde stood by the edge of the pond. There was a mound of sand that someone had put there. The water lapped ever so slightly. He stared down into it. There were fish. Their silvery backs flicked right and left, right and left. How he wanted to catch one. It should be easy enough, he thought, to just catch one with your hands. Why couldn't you? Why didn't anyone ever? He'd caught minnows and crayfish and salamanders and frogs in the creek at home. Why not a fish? He could even feel it slippery between his palms. He took off his shoes and stepped into the water. He could see the plants on the bottom. He let the fish gather around his feet. They flicked right and left, right and left. He squatted down ever so carefully to get his hands nearer for when he made the plunge. He thrust his hands downward. He felt the edge of a slippery back, the soft, quick brush of a tail. It was just one edge of a fish he had touched. He hadn't even managed to get his hands around the whole thing.

*

Coralie had invited Lu upstairs. "I have the most incredible dress," she said, "you have to try it on. It'll look just incredible on you."

Lu followed her into the room.

The bedroom was cluttered with things, the mattress on the floor. "It's a dump," Coralie said. "We live in this beautiful house and then of course we get the dump. You know?" Lu didn't answer. "You know?" Coralie asked again, staring into Lu's face, openly, directly, like a child or an animal would.

"Yeah," Lu said. She gazed around, then out the window. "It's not so bad. I like it."

"You like it? You do? You really do?" Coralie looked around, as if seeing the place for the first time. Even though she had grown up all over Europe, she had an easy-going American accent. "Well, I tried to fix it up." There was a Spanish shawl with tassels hanging from a nail on the wall. She reached out and tugged it. "You see? You see this? I put this here." She shrugged.

"That's nice," Lu said.

"Lewis doesn't do anything. I have to do everything." Coralie looked around. It seemed she'd forgotten the dress completely. Her eyes fell on a sheaf of papers on the table.

"Oh God," she said, "I'm working on this poem. Do you want to hear it?"

Lu shrugged and nodded at the same time.

"You have to hear it. I was working on it all yesterday. It's just, you know when you feel something's larger than yourself? Well, this poem is larger than myself. It just came out of me, you know. It was like having a baby. Or, I don't know, maybe not a baby but like a small wolf instead of a baby."

"God," Lu said.

"Yeah, that's an image, isn't it? Maybe I should put that image in the poem. Here, let me read it to you."

Lu twisted around. She felt uncomfortable. She didn't want to have to stand there and listen and then say something afterward.

"Wait, wait, but you know what," Coralie said, "I can't read it like this. I have to put something else on. I'm planning to read it, you know, if I ever finish it, at this poetry festival. I know the guy who runs it. I told him I wanted to read something, 'an epic poem,' I said. 'Epic'? Can you believe I said that? Anyway, this is what I'm going to wear." She took a long cream dress out of the closet.

Coralie took off her shorts—she had white cotton underwear on—then her shirt. Lu watched, then looked away. When she looked back, Coralie had pulled the dress down over her head. It fit her snugly.

"What do you think?" she asked.

"Nice," Lu said.

"Okay, here. Let me read the poem. It's not finished, okay? This is just the first part."

She began to read. It was a love story, about Lewis, a narrative poem, beginning with the scene when they had first met. Every once in a while, Coralie stopped to point out a word choice. The poem went on and on. Lu sat down on the edge of the armchair. She had a view out the window. She listened and looked out the window.

Finally, the poem ended.

"Did you like it?" Coralie asked.

Lu nodded.

"You did? You really did?"

"Yeah," Lu said. She felt very tired. She got up from her chair.

"Oh, wait," Coralie said, "I wanted to show you that dress. Oh God, I forgot all about it. I just like so much talking to you."

Coralie went back to the closet, plunged her head into it and began looking through everything. She pulled her head out again.

"I always knew we'd get along," she said, then plunged her head back in. "You know," she said, her head emerging again, her arms still in the closet, "I actually really almost never had a female friend." She waited. "Have you?"

Lu shrugged and then nodded. "I have one or two."

Coralie gazed at her for a long moment—too long, Lu felt—and then put her head back in the closet.

"Here!" Coralie said. She'd found the dress. It was sky blue, with a bell skirt. "Come on," she said to Lu, "try it on."

Now Lu had to take her clothes off in front of Coralie. Coralie stared with her large brown eyes. Lu turned away, shyly, trying to hide. But when she turned back and looked in the mirror, she saw that Coralie was right. The dress did look wonderful on her.

*

Then it came true, Tuck's dream. He was crouched again by the study door. His grandfather came out and saw him.

"Hey there, little guy." His grandfather couldn't distinguish any of their names. "Come, I want to show you something."

He turned and went back into his study. Tuck couldn't believe his luck. He hesitantly followed. A little passage led between the wall and the bookshelves, crammed with things. Then you turned and entered the room itself. There was a draftsman's table tilted upwards, piles of maps, scrolls of plans. On the shelves were comic books, mechanic's magazines, folders and files, a collection of ski wax, a shelf of exquisitely made Japanese toys. The files were full of clippings and were labeled by project, ski lift, rice pond, snow. Tuck had always known it was an enchanted place. Now he could see for himself.

His grandfather was kneeling down, tinkering with what looked like a little model machine.

Tuck knelt down too. He knew that his grandfather could operate all kinds of machines, farm machines, technical machines. That's how half his finger got chopped off, in a wheat thresher. His grandfather was also an excellent skier—he floated down the slopes, arms out; he was famous for that, skiing without poles—and a sailor—he always won the prize in the yearly Lenox race.

Now his grandfather sprang up again. This was how he moved. He always seemed to have springs on his feet.

"Let's go," he said.

Tuck followed him out, back down the passageway and out of the study, through the kitchen—his grandfather sneaked two sugar cubes from the bowl, gave one to Tuck—and out the door toward the garage. This was where the most part of the projects were collected, the sailboat hull, the hay-drying machine. To position the hay-drying machine just right, he'd cut open one whole wall of the barn.

But his grandfather was interested in something else today. "Look," he said. It was a contraption, boxlike, a larger version of what he had been fiddling with in the study, the miniature machine. "Now we're going to see if it works."

*

Lonnie wore her sweat suit and her glasses and had a clipboard in her hand.

"Okay, okay, we've called a meeting," she said. Sam, Lewis, and Rita were gathered with her in the dining room. Rita sat at the table eating a plate of liver and bean sprouts sprinkled heavily with yeast. Lewis was covered with grass from mowing. Lonnie looked at Sam. "No, Sam, you should start. You should say it. Okay, well, I will."

The dining room adjoined the front hall through a wide arched doorway. Maeve could almost stay in place now on the unicycle, just moving back and forth slightly. She watched from the front hall, treading. There she goes again, she thought, looking at Lonnie, always making a scene.

"When's Fran getting here?" Lonnie asked.

"Who knows? She's driving up from the city," Lewis said.

"Should we wait for her?" Lonnie asked

"No, no, forget it," Sam said.

"What about Christopher?"

"I told him," Sam said. "He laughed in my face."

"May's not coming at all now. She called," Lewis said. "There's a Tompkins family affair. And then she's going to the Canaan Islands."

Rita shuddered. "She's packing the most ridiculous clothes. She's sure to get raped in an instant."

Maeve turned, shifting her weight just slightly and angled into the library. Out of sight now, she could still hear.

"Okay," Lonnie said. "It doesn't matter. The meeting is for the people who are here. The point of this meeting is that unless you do something now, you're going to have to end up selling the whole place off. Right? That's clear. No one's generating any money. So the idea is to figure out what to do. First let's go through all the things that have been tried. Lewis?"

"Hmm. Okay, well, there was the idea of the lumber mill. Then there were the turkeys, the rice pond. For many years, Dad wanted to start a ski resort up Monument Mountain. He designed it and everything. This was before they knew how to make snow. He was very excited about that project, did all sorts of experiments. He was sure it could be manufactured with dry ice."

Lonnie was taking notes. She paused. "Okay, but whoever thought these things were going to make money?" she asked.

"Dad did," Lewis said. "There was the farming. The latest thing is the fish pond. That's Chris's enterprise. And the tenant houses."

"Now, the tenant houses are interesting," Lonnie said.

As they were speaking, Christopher showed up surreptitiously. "I think you neglected to mention the outpatient project."

"Oh, yeah, that was Mum's project," Lewis said.

"Hmm," Rita said.

"We're very glad you're here, Christopher," Lonnie said.

Christopher ignored this. "When she learned how much they were paying to be locked up, Mum took it into her head to take in the outpatients from the Warren Psychiatric Institute right down the road. It's a very chic place."

"And how did that work out?" Lonnie asked.

"He-he-he. There were some interesting results—Coralie, for example. And May, our eldest sister, married another of the patients, her first marriage. Too bad he tried to strangle her."

"Uh-huh. And in terms of profit?"

Everyone looked at Rita.

"Hmm. I have the figures somewhere," she said.

As with all greyhounds when they get older, the dog Milton's back legs were weak. He was standing out in the hall. His back legs sunk down.

"Okay, let's return to the tenant houses. How many are there?" Lonnie asked.

"Eight," Lewis said.

Lonnie noted this down. "Good. And what are the rents?"

"Nothing. No one pays anything." Christopher said, then went out again, laughing.

Lonnie persisted. "Why does no one pay anything?"

Clyde ran headlong into the dining room, tripping and falling over the dog, then getting back up again, as if he hadn't even noticed.

"Dad! Dad! I saw a huge fish!"

"Really?" Sam said.

Clyde nodded emphatically. "Enormous."

Lewis knelt down. "You did? You saw it? The prehistoric fish?" His face, usually so placid, lit up, his pale blue eyes, like the grandfather's, gleaming.

"Yeah, he came right toward me," Clyde said.

Lewis laughed. "That's what he does. He's been doing that for twenty years. He comes right at you. He's either very hungry or very mad."

"I know that fish," a voice said. It was their aunt Fran, just arriving, standing now in the door of the dining room. She made an astonishing figure. She wore striped tights, a short animal-print dress and had long red hair in pigtails. As she spoke, she held her head back, eyes nearly closed.

Then, out of the blue, she leapt forward, sweeping her arms from one side to the other. "Swoosh!"

Clyde jumped back. He didn't even understand exactly what that was supposed to be—the fish? But it gave him an idea.

"Hey," he said to Fran, "will you do Goldilocks and the Three Bears?"

Fran leapt up onto the dining room table. She started sawing her elbows and kicking her legs. "This is the story of a girl named Goldilocks and—the Three Bears. Cha-cha-cha." Clyde watched, wide-eyed. It was even more remarkable than what he'd remembered. Even better, the song went on and on. "So Goldilocks she woke up and broke up the party and she beat it out of there. Cha—cha—cha."

"Awwright, geez, Fran," Sam said, "we're trying to have a meeting."

She put her head back, her eyes opened just a crack. "Oh, I see, a meeting about what?"

"About the place, what's going to happen."

"This family is in deep shit," Lonnie said.

"Uh-huh, I see. And who, may I ask, are you?" Fran said, still standing on the table.

Lonnie blushed.

"This is Lonnie," Sam said.

"Oh, Lonnie, Lonnie. Oh, your girlfriend, right. Getting right down to brass tacks, I see. And, uh, let's see, do you work as some kind of financial advisor?"

"No," Lonnie said, dazzled, blushing. "I just—well—"

"She knows what she's talking about," Sam said. "At least she's got a fucking clue, which this family doesn't. I mean, do you realize what Dad's been up to?"

The teenager, Alex, wandered into the front hall with his headphones on. He stopped, looked in on the scene in the dining room with Fran up on the table and Lonnie with her clipboard, pulled his headphones off, and leaned against the doorway to listen.

"Well, I guess he figures it was his fortune in the first place," Fran said. "He can do what he wants with it."

"Soon this will all be gone. Soon there will be nothing left," Rita said to no one.

"Exactly!" Lonnie said. "That's right. The idea is to figure out a strategy, either to make that not happen or to figure out what you're going to do when it does."

Fran climbed down from the table, knees and elbows jutting out. "Did any of you consider the possibility that the guy's a genius? Did any of you ever even think of that?"

"Heyyy!" It was Reb again, "the engineer," appearing from the other side through the swinging pantry door. "Listen guys, you have to come outside and see this. We've got the model set up by the pond. Test trial number one."

He disappeared again. Alex, his pants legs dragging on the floor, began to follow at a leisurely pace. Others in the room seemed to be also shifting in that direction.

"Wait, everybody, hold on," Lonnie said, her hands up in the air. "Let's hear from the younger generation. You, you, Alex!"

Alex turned back.

"What do you think about all this?" Lonnie asked.

"People say that the individual is becoming extinct," Alex said. "But I think, along with Marx, that the individual has yet to appear, the true individual."

Fran approached him, standing very near. "Oh, yeah, then what about us? These people here? What about Papa? Is he not an individual?"

"No, he's not. He's a completely determined social type. His politics, tastes, self-delusions, are all determined by his class. We don't even know yet what an individual looks like. We're just beginning to see."

Alex put the headphones back on.

"And I suppose you're the first individual?" Fran shouted at him, hands on her hips.

Seeing her shouting, he pulled his headphones off again. "What?"

"I suppose you're the first individual?" she said.

He smiled. He was standing right under one of the portraits, a young man in a high velvet collar, who looked exactly like him. "Maybe," he said. "Or"—he pointed at Lonnie—"maybe she is." He put the headphones back on.

Fran stamped her foot, infuriated. "Bad idea, bad idea. Remember that, Fran. Coming home, always a bad idea."

*

They had put the contraption on a set of boards with wheels and dragged it out to the pond. The light was just beginning to fail. The dark leaves of the copper beech were rustling. The feathery plants swayed on the bottom of the pond. Tuck's grandfather knelt down, fiddling with the contraption, which looked like a small power plant. Reb cleared reeds away from the pond's edge. Tuck stood near, his thumb hooked in his belt loop.

A few people began to filter out of the house, Lonnie among them, walking between Lewis and Sam.

"Maybe he *is* a genius," Lonnie said.

"Shit," Sam said.

Lewis shrugged. "I wish I could believe it. There just always seems to be something wrong."

"Like what?" Lonnie asked.

"Well, for example, Dad's father was a gold digger. He went to Alaska looking for gold and then came up with this plan to import horses. There were no horses in Alaska. It was a good idea, only he forgot one thing: Horses need hay. There was nothing for them to eat. He put them in the boat, got them all there, and then the poor suckers died of starvation."

They approached. The contraption was working. Something at least was happening. Lights were blinking. There was a whirring sound.

Their grandfather, Walt, was standing, hands poised, right near the machine. Lonnie stopped and watched him for a moment, clearly impressed. "Oh, Walt," she said, approaching, wiggling ever so slightly, "you're the first real inventor I've met in my life."

Sam, annoyed, turned to Rita, who was standing barefoot in the grass. "Mum, where are your shoes?" he asked.

She looked up at him. He was struck by how her face looked in that moment, suddenly fresh and young. "I decided long ago that I was a pantheist," she said.

Then the whirring stopped. Walt and Reb both descended on the machine. They started fiddling. They flipped a switch.

Clyde ran out of the house, looking baffled. Tuck raised an arm: "Over here!"

"What is it?" Clyde asked, breathless, as he arrived.

Tuck touched the contraption. "A water-changing machine."

*

There were the ball gowns in the attic, the ball gowns! Once there had been parties in the house. Once, Lu thought, the house had been full of the swish, swish sound of these gowns. The climbing and descending of the stairs, the backs of the gowns furling like water over the ledge of each step.

*

Christopher looked around at his family seated at the dinner table. His eyes swum behind his glasses. Rita wore a purple dress, Walt a white shirt and black pants.

Lonnie took another slice of lamb from the platter that was being passed around. "It's as if they're living, I don't know, four or five generations in the past," she whispered to the teenager, Alex, who was sitting beside her, his head-phones down around his neck.

Coralie had insisted that Lu sit beside her. "You're the only person I can talk to here," she had said. Lu had felt flattered and a bit nervous too. Now Coralie leaned over and said into Lu's ear, "Lewis and I are getting divorced."

Lu turned to her, shocked. "You are?" Her parents had also gotten divorced.

Coralie laughed. "Yes, we are." Lewis, sitting across the table from them, looked up. "I just told her that we're getting divorced," Coralie said. She turned back to Lu. "We're not even married, but we're getting divorced."

"Someone gave me that South American book, *One Hundred Years of Solitude*," Rita said, "but when I got to the part where he sells his mule for a set of magnets, I couldn't read it anymore."

Christopher cleared his throat, as if irritated. "I gave you that book," he said. He turned to Alex, without looking at him. "So there, Alex, what are you up to?" he asked. "You want to write?"

"Not particularly," Alex said.

Christopher ignored this as an answer. Of course he wanted to write. Everyone in that family wanted to write.

"Have you read all of Shakespeare?" Christopher asked. Alex shrugged. "Some."

"Oh, oh, oh, you have to read Shakespeare. Or at least the major plays. *Lear,* have you read *Lear?* You must've read *Lear.* And *Hamlet?*"

Christopher went through them. His glasses were thick. He was dressed as usual just like his father, in black pants and a white shirt. His hair was combed back and ended in curls at his neck.

"And what about the Russians? You must have read the Russians." He went through the Russians. He asked Alex about *The Brothers Karamazov.*

"You haven't read *The Brothers Karamazov?* Oh, oh, oh." Was it a stutter, this repetition? "Well, yes," Christopher said, "it's true, *The Brothers Karamazov* is a scary book." He laughed and looked around the table. "It makes you want to kill yourself, or at least kill someone."

"I really can't stand it," Fran said, interrupting. "Everywhere I go in the city, people think I'm a movie star. It happened again just the other day. People stopped on the street and stared at me. And the cabdrivers. I can't take a cab. They all want to sleep with me."

"Oh," Rita murmured, glancing down at her plate.

"But I have come to at least one conclusion," Fran said. "I've decided that I only like black men."

Rita got up.

"Mum, where are you going?" Sam asked.

"I forgot to water the pumpkin squash," Rita said.

Sam looked at Lonnie, who looked back at him hard. "No, no, Mum, you have to stay."

Christopher lit a cigarette and leaned back. No one else was allowed to smoke in that house, only him, because something had gone wrong, because he lived in a shack in the woods. "You know," he said, taking a puff, "there's some evidence that this family is descended from Alexander the Great." For a moment, everyone stopped, listened.

"That must mean," Alex said, "that somewhere along the line we're descended from Achilles." He paused, smiled slightly.

"Why's that?" Fran asked.

"Because Alexander the Great claimed descent from Achilles."

For an instant, everyone held his or her breath, knew it was absurd, half believed.

"Walt," Lonnie said, turning to him flirtatiously, breaking the spell. "I think your children want to talk to you."

She looked over at Sam. He turned as if to address the table, but hedged. He opened his mouth, but it was clear he was going to stutter. His mouth was open but nothing came out.

Lonnie, watching, then spoke herself. "Walt," she said, "we all love and admire you very much, but we have something to tell you. Your family thinks that you need to be declared incompetent. They need to take the money out of your hands."

There was a silence. Walt glanced at Rita, truly surprised. She looked down. He glanced at the others. Tuck couldn't bear it and sank down on his knees under the table.

Christopher suddenly laughed. "Brilliant, brilliant," he said. "This is absurd."

But Lonnie persisted. "Otherwise there won't be anything left for them, don't you see?"

"She's right, you know, she's right," Sam burst out. "For example, I'm gonna want out. I'm telling you that now. I'm eventually gonna want out. And May will too. How're the rest of you going to buy out our share?"

"The winters are so long and dark," Rita said. "I feel that I've lived here my whole life, but I haven't."

"Okay, all right, Sam, one thing at a time," Lonnie said, hands up near her face.

"No, but that's the reality," Sam said, looking around.

"So you're saying you're going to demand your share of the house from Mum and Dad?" Fran asked, her chin jutting out.

"No, no, of course, it would be after they're gone."

"I'm not worried about the next life," Rita murmured. "I just want to get through this one as gracefully as possible."

Fran looked at Rita's plate, alarmed. Instead of what the rest of them were eating, lamb, there was a pile of soybeans. "Mum, what are you eating? Why are you eating that stuff?"

Coralie stood, taking a candle out of the candelabra. "*'Aujourd'hui, maman est morte. Ou peut-être hier, je ne sais pas. J'ai reçu un télégramme de l'asile.'*" (Mother died today. Or maybe yesterday, I don't know. I received a telegram from the home.) Lewis moved to stop her. Coralie put her hand out toward him. "Wait, wait, let me finish," she said, in a completely different voice, pleading, than the one she had been reciting in. "We memorized the whole first part at school." She went on: "*''Mère décédée. Enterrement demain.*

Sentiments distingués."'" (Mother deceased. Burial tomorrow. Respectfully yours.)

Fran put her head back, eyes closed, and let out a soundless openmouthed laugh.

"You like it?" Coralie asked. "That was *L'Étranger,* the opening. You know it?"

Christopher suddenly stood up, irritably. "This house will be sold over my dead body," he said. Everyone looked at him, surprised. No one had thought he even cared.

Reb rushed through the swinging pantry door. "Dudes, listen, the machine's acting up. I think the freaking thing's sinking into the pond!"

Walt leapt to his feet. Tuck scrambled out from under the table and ran after him.

The dog, Milton, wanted to follow. He tried to lift himself, dropped, tried again, dropped.

"You're going to lose everything!" Lonnie yelled.

Fran turned to her. "Anyway," Fran said, "what's it to you?"

❋

The children were getting ready for bed. Their grandmother slept at the end of the hall, near their bedroom. In their minds, her room was all purple and lavender, full of vapors. They'd been in it so infrequently, maybe even just once. She had a waterbed under the windows. They remembered the feeling of rolling around on that waterbed, the humps of water rising and falling like waves, and the fogged windows, the purple walls.

Their grandfather slept downstairs in a small, undistinguished room off the kitchen in what looked like a hospital bed. He'd moved down there when the waterbed had arrived. But not just because of that.

✳

Maeve sat by the open window. Lu was over there in the bed they shared, the cheek with the mole on it up. Clyde was curled up in a ball on the chaise longue, Tuck in the corner in the single bed. She looked outside. She could see the contraption out by the pond, hunched there, waiting, half sunk in the water. She pictured the flower she'd seen that day in the garden, the pumpkin squash, its scalloped edges and ghostly pale throat. She wondered if it closed up in the night.

The night. How soft and delicious and dark it was. The cool, watery air, the moonlight lighting everything. She longed to wander out in the moonlight across the yard. Or down the drive and out across the lower fields or up the mountain road. The land goes on and on. Everywhere are shacks, barns, houses, log cabins, swamps and woods and meadows and the great hump of the mountain. No, there's too much. You'd have to fly over. If only you could fly over in the moonlight.

But she paused. She seemed to hear something, a breathing, a sighing. What was it? She leaned out the window and listened further. The pond water lapping? The wind in the pines? As if the whole world was letting out one last gasp.

DRESSING UP

Just in time for cocktails!" our mother's mother, Gran, says, obviously exasperated, coming to meet us out on the drive. We were supposed to be there for lunch. Now, dressed in her cocktail clothes—white pants, a silk smock, gold shoes and jewelry—after perfunctory kisses hello (she's irritated) and the quickest sizing-up of our mother's boyfriend extricating himself from the car (he's enormous, dwarfing our grandmother, covered with hair), she's already heading back to the house. "I have a guest!" she says. Her step's a little wobbly. She places her feet somewhat far apart. "He's rich!" she calls over her shoulder. "Recently divorced!"

Our mother, her eyes already more squinted than usual, busies herself unloading the bags. We four kids pile out of the car. Clyde reels around on the pavement, his sweaty hair plastered to his face. He's been sleeping. Lu has a headache because she's been trying to read. She presses her palm to the side of her head. Tuck and I have been playing bloody knuckles. We both have one very sore hand. Each hauling a suitcase, we straggle inside.

We visit our grandmother twice a year, once in winter, once in summer. This is our summer visit, mid-July. Our grandmother's house on Long Island is flat, one level, with red-tiled floors, and divided into adult and children's quarters. In the children's quarters are two bedrooms furnished with twin or bunk beds, above which hang sets of engravings of white men chasing Indians or the reverse. Lu and I, the oldest, always take the room with the twin beds covered with blue-and-white-striped bed covers, while Tuck and Clyde are in the bunk beds.

For cocktails at our grandmother's we always have to dress. This is by far the fanciest event in our lives. Lu and I open our suitcases and take out our fanciest clothes. Our mother always brings her dress-up clothes, too, but they're still hippie clothes. With our grandmother, she's always between obedience and rebellion. Is our mother's boy-friend, Chester, going to change? We've never seen him wearing anything but what he has on now: blue jeans, a T-shirt and lace-up boots. He keeps his hair in a pony-tail. We first saw him speaking at antinuclear rallies, where they introduced him as Dr. Kemp. Even now when we hear him talking, his low full voice coming out of his beard, it sounds like he's speaking into a microphone.

I put on my dress and sandals. Lu does too. We look at ourselves in the mirror. As always, we're worried that our grandmother will find us dirty or without manners or not dressed right.

There's a step up into the part of the house where the adults reign, the dining room, with its gleaming appoint-ments, the living room, the bedrooms farther back. The kitchen is hidden away, shunned, like in a restaurant. We never go there. Cocktails are served in the living room. Everything is slick and polished, the cocktail table, the cocktail tray. Our grandmother doesn't own particularly valuable things. What she can't abide are nicks and stains. Anything nicked or stained is quickly thrown away. Two porcelain elephants stand by the fireplace. Through the liv-ing room windows, you can look out and see the swimming pool, shaped like a kidney. To one side of the pool is a dog kennel filled with spotted hunting dogs.

Kneeling on the floor, dressed in our fancy clothes, we gobble down all the hors d'oeuvres, scallops wrapped in bacon, tiny sausages in rolls, shrimp dipped in cocktail sauce, clams on the half shell.

"My Gawd!" our grandmother says in her mid-Atlantic drawl, having looked away and then back to find the plates empty. She, as usual, is horrified at our appetites.

Our mother and her boyfriend sit on the couch. Our mother wears an Indian dress with fringes on it. Chester has put on a button-down shirt. He's not a drinker but a pot smoker—he grows his own plants—but he's taken a gin and tonic all the same. Our mother has one too. Suddenly, after admiring our grandmother's slender gold cocktail shoes, I glance down and see our mother's feet, her toenails full of dirt from working in the garden. I look up quickly at our grandmother's face. Has she seen?

Our grandmother lights a cigarette.

"Alec was a star athlete at Princeton," she says, referring to her guest.

Alec laughs. He has a straight perfectly shaped nose. He's debonair, just what our grandmother likes, a man who drinks cocktails, wears clean pressed clothes, combs his pressed wet-looking hair back from his forehead. "You put the left-hand shot in the right-hand corner," he says.

Our mother's squinted gaze is just polite. Of course we know that she'd never like this man, not in a million years. But our grandmother doesn't see it.

Chester leans forward, taking a long abrupt sip of the drink he doesn't want.

This gives me an idea. "Gran," I say, when she gets back, "can we have Shirley Temples?" She's the person who introduced us to Shirley Temples.

"Of course, darling. Alec, fix the children Shirley Temples."

Alec gets up quickly to oblige.

"We were just talking about the Jockey Club when you arrived, Faye," our grandmother says, "It seems your old beau Roger has been trying to get in."

"Of course we didn't let him," Alec says. The cocktail tray has wheels. He's standing in front of it, back turned, fixing our drinks.

"Why not?" our mother asks.

"Well," Alec says, turning, "to start with, he's an activist."

"An activist?" our mother says. She laughs. "Since when is Roger an activist?" She turns to Chester. "You should see this guy."

"Oh, that's right," Alec says, as if mildly embarrassed, addressing Chester. "Because you, I understand, are the real thing."

Chester smiles, dryly amused.

"Chester also does research," our mother says. "He's a radiation chemist." It's not clear what she means, where she's heading with this. She looks irritated, distracted, as if she herself doesn't know what she wants.

"Oh, really? What sort of research?" Alec asks, distributing the Shirley Temples. I eat my cherry right away. Lu dunks hers, turning her whole glass rosy.

"Radiation tests. We study the effects of radiation, even low-level radiation, on thyroid function and mental development. The results are indisputable, not to mention the higher rates of infant mortality, miscarriages and deaths by cancer in areas surrounding a nuclear power plant."

"Gawd." Our grandmother finds anything to do with study or the academic life profoundly boring. She holds out her glass to Alec. Her drink is a bullshot: beef broth,

Worcestershire sauce, vodka, and lime. Alec's drinking the same. Still at the bar, he refreshes both their glasses.

"We're not even talking about accidents here," Chester goes on. "That's a whole other story. But of course it's all covered up. The figures the government was spouting following the Three Mile Island meltdown were way off."

"They left," our grandmother says to Alec, the judgment clear but unspoken behind the words. "Faye took the children out of school."

It was actually Chester who came in the middle of the day to take us out of school. He said there had been an accident at a nuclear power plant not far away and we had to get out of there fast. At home, our mother told us to pack a few things we really loved, because we might not ever come back to this house again.

"Why wouldn't we?" Lu asked. She was wearing by chance that day her "Stop Nuclear Power" T-shirt.

"Because," our mother said, "we don't know what's going to happen. We'll just have to see."

I couldn't think of what to bring. I looked through the things I had—my terrarium? My cactus plants? I packed some polished rocks. They didn't take much room. I could hold all four of them in the palm of my hand.

It was a hasty departure. Within an hour we were gone.

"Hold your breath," Lu said as we were going out to the car.

"Why?" I asked.

"Because the air's poisonous now."

I held my breath between the front door and the car.

We drove south with our mother. Chester, not trusting the official meters, stayed behind to take radiation readings downwind of the plant. He would join us when he was done. The landscape was unfamiliar: Maryland, green horse pastures, white fences, Virginia. As we drove, we kept the radio on for news of the accident.

"Why aren't the other kids at school leaving too?" Tuck asked.

"Because they don't know," our mother said. "Nobody knows the truth. The government always lies about these things." She was in the passenger's seat. She turned away, then back. "But everything might also be just fine."

We drove all day. By nightfall, we had made it as far as Tennessee. We stopped in a little town at the base of the Blue Ridge Mountains, checked into a motel, and went to a restaurant to eat. In the restaurant, there was a row of deer heads with full antlers over the bar.

We all slept in one room in the motel, our mother and Lu in the bed, the rest of us on the floor in our sleeping bags. The next morning, when we stepped out, we saw that there was a plastic swimming pool in the parking lot with a high curved slide. We hadn't noticed it the night before in the dark. Lu, Tuck, and I went over to look. But there was no water in the pool. Its sides were plastered with fallen brown leaves.

The days went by slowly. With the pool empty, there wasn't much to do around the motel. In front of it were a parking lot and a road. In back was a fence and behind the fence a brick building. If you went around the other side, you saw that in the brick building were a sneaker shop and a liquor store. We loitered in the parking lot. We played cards. Our mother called Chester to tell him where we were. She listened to the radio and watched the news on the motel TV. It was funny to see our mother watching TV. We didn't have a TV at our house. We kids also watched, hypnotized. But there was hardly any more news about the accident.

A week later, Chester joined us. He had been supposed to appear on TV himself, following the accident, but his appearance had been canceled at the last minute when they found out what he was going to say. He made a lot of calls from the motel room. They were planning the next big anti-nuke rally and he was going to speak.

We spoke to our father on the phone. Our mother took us on wildflower walks in the hills. A guide told us all about the mountain flowers. We were missing school. I worried about the tests I wasn't taking and the prizes I would now never win. At night, lying on the floor in my sleeping bag, unable to sleep, I pictured our house perched on the hill, empty, its windows staring out. The trees around it were all dead, the creek below dry and brown.

But when we finally did come back, everything was still alive. The creek was rippling, the apple trees in bloom. The blossoms smelled sweet as ever. But were they poisoned? Would we be able to eat the fruit? I walked around looking, not touching things.

Our grandmother turns to Lu. "How long were you away from school?"

But Lu doesn't budge. She's on our mother's side. She shrugs. Our grandmother, annoyed, turns to me.

"Three weeks," I say.

"Three weeks!" she says, reporting, triumphant.

"Wasn't that a bit alarmist?" Alec asks.

"Well, actually, no," Chester says. "Not if you knew what was really going on." He begins to recite figures. He looks gigantic, imperturbable. His voice is deep, far-off, as if he were once again addressing crowds. The hors d'oeuvres are gone. Outside in the dark, the pool is glowing. There are lights on the floor of it. I picture jumping in, the way the water jets stream out at you underneath the surface. It would be cool but not too cool. It would be nice to step out of our fancy clothes.

*

"Now, Clyde," our grandmother asks, "what would your favorite meal be?" We've moved into the dining room. The dining room table is made of dark polished wood. You can see the knots far beneath the polish gleaming. The silverware feels large and heavy in our hands. "Starting with the appetizer." Although the food she serves is rich and delicious, a crabmeat appetizer, sole with potatoes steeped in butter, our grandmother eats almost nothing herself, a hard-boiled egg at lunchtime, a few bites at dinner. "You can choose both a meat and a fish." Clyde doesn't know what she's talking about. "And then the dessert." She hasn't had dessert, we've heard, in thirty years. She used to be chubby, our mother tells us, when our mother was growing up, but since then our grandmother decided, with the same relentless determination with which she holds her opinions, never to be "fat" again.

"Pork chops," Clyde says.

Lu starts laughing.

"Good for you," Alec says. "A meat-and-potatoes man." He seems to be drunker. There's sweat on his brow. Both he and our grandmother have brought their drinks to the table.

Our grandmother turns to our mother. "So, Faye dear, tell us about the addition. Faye's building a wonderful new addition," she explains to Alec. "She's been living for years with a dirt floor in the kitchen. Dirt! Can you imagine? You dropped an egg and there it was. There was nothing to do but rub it into the dirt." She rubs her gold sandal in a circle on the floor.

"I really enjoy the countryside," Alec says to our mother. "I have a country place myself."

"You do?" our mother asks.

"Sure! I like to go out walking or I shoot. I've got a little firing range set up."

"You hunt?" our mother asks.

"No, not much. But I like to shoot."

"That's wonderful," our grandmother says.

Our mother persists. "Why is that wonderful?"

She's thinking of the hunters who come onto our land and who, one year, shot our dogs.

"Well, shooting is wonderful, of course!" our grandmother says. "Everyone should know how to shoot."

Our grandmother has these implacable rules. Everyone should drink. A woman should marry rich. Everyone should know how to shoot. Sometimes in the afternoon she takes us out to shoot clay pigeons with her. She wears tan pants with leather bits sewn on them in the front. Standing there, her blond hair pulled back in a headband, she looks down the sights of her rifle, one eye squinted, and fires. Or she takes us to the horse races where we place bets. Once a visit we go with her to see her jeweler. We peer out into the yard by the pool to see if our mother wants to come. But she's not interested. She never wears jewelry anyway. We're all dressed up, the best we can do, to go out with our grandmother. "Bye, Faye," our grandmother calls. What's our mother doing? Is she digging up the plants? Is she painting? She has her easel set up, so she must be painting. Her hands are dirty. She wears cut-off shorts. She has paint on her legs. Although in our normal life our mother is always dressed like this and always outdoors working with her hands, in this moment we look at her from where we're standing by the glass door with our grandmother's implacable gaze. Why doesn't our mother clean herself up, wear some decent clothes? It's an embarrassment. What's she thinking, behaving like this?

Our grandmother's car is dark green and shiny, with monograms on the doors. Once in town, we follow her, tap-tap, along the sidewalk. She wears beautifully cut pants, low flat shoes. She's tan—she always seems to be tan—and smells of perfume. We're allowed to choose something, a stone for a pendant, nothing too precious, or maybe a watch. Then we follow her, tap-tap, back along the sidewalk to the car.

We're just finishing the chocolate mousse. They're talking about our aunt's wedding, our mother's sister, the second time around, which we all went to a month or so ago. "Why couldn't they just have a normal wedding?" our grandmother asks. "Hmm? A normal wedding, a lovely white cake?"

The wedding was outside and our mother acted as priest. She stood with two tall reeds stuck in the ground on either side of her. Then everyone sat down in a circle on the ground. A musician played the sitar. A woman in a green dress, our aunt's best friend, sang.

Our mother stiffens. She doesn't say anything. Then she does. "Because they didn't want that, Mum."

Our grandmother looks at her, as if not understanding. Blank, child eyes. The thing is not understandable.

Chester is quiet. This is what happens when he starts to get in a bad mood. He has a dry sort of humor when he's feeling all right, but when he gets in a bad mood he turns silent. He sinks further and further, often not speaking for days. Our mother stays clear of him and tells us to too.

Our grandmother turns to Alec. "And then they served pasta." She says "pasta" with a short a, like "cat."

"What's wrong with pasta?" Alec asks, already amused.

Our grandmother takes another sip of her drink. She has that light in her eyes. This is when she starts getting outrageous. "What's wrong with it? What *is* it? Flour and water, flour and water!"

Alec laughs appreciatively.

Chester gets up from the table. "Excuse me," he says, and leaves.

Alec turns and smiles at our mother, raising his glass. "The face that launched a thousand ships," he says.

Our mother's flattered. She can't help it. Having grown up in a house with girls—her father died young—she can never get enough attention from men.

"You should see Faye's work," our grandmother says. "She's a marvelous painter."

What our mother won't do, though, is please her mother. She stands up abruptly to clear the plates.

"No, no, Faye, leave it," our grandmother says.

I've been thinking again about the pool. I can tell Tuck and Lu have been eyeing it too. Now Tuck asks what's in all our heads. "Mom, can we go swimming?"

Back in our rooms, we shed our fancy clothes as fast as we can and pull on our bathing suits. Racing each other, we dash back through the house, out the sliding glass doors, and jump into the pool. The jets along the sides shoot out silver bubbles. It's bright blue, deliciously cool. Tuck and Clyde play with the jets. Lu likes to dive down and skim the bottom.

Soon we're taking turns climbing out of the pool, running and doing dives or leaps of different kinds. I step behind a set of low bushes, thinking I'll add a variation by leaping over the bushes and then taking my dive. But there's something there in the dark, a long shape on the grass. It's a person, Chester, lying down. He's smoking a joint, looking up at the sky. He turns his head and sees me, but doesn't say anything. I don't say anything, either.

A little while later, our grandmother and Alec step out of the house, fresh drinks in hand. Our grandmother, it seems, is on a roll.

"Charles Manson was a sex symbol, of course he was!"

Alec's delighted. "But, Rosie, really, how can you say that?"

"It's obvious! Just look at all those beautiful gurls he had."

Alec, chortling, totters over to pee in the bushes.

Our mother comes outside too and looks around for Chester. She calls out his name.

Suddenly Chester gets up, right near where Alec is peeing—I can see his dark, towering shape—and, silent and furious, walks away.

Our mother starts to follow him, but Alec, returning, cuts her off. Shirt untucked, standing on the flagstones around the pool, he does a little dance step in front of her. "The one-step two-step Fred Astaire," he says.

Our grandmother laughs, her whole body collapsing entirely, charmingly, the way our mother's does, too, when she laughs. But our mother's not laughing now. She looks confused. It's as if she can't afford the luxury of frolicking. She wants a world where things mean something.

The night air has turned cool.

"I'm going to ask," Lu says to me, shivering. Beside her, Clyde is clinging to the edge of the pool, teeth chattering.

Our grandmother and Alec are now sitting at an iron table out on the flagstones. Lu pulls herself up out of the water and walks over to them. .

"The face that launched a thousand ships," Alec says as she arrives.

"Gran," Lu says, ignoring him, "can we take a bath?"

"Of course, darling," our grandmother says.

Dripping and shivering, the four of us follow our grandmother into the house. She walks ahead of us jerkily, placing her feet far apart. We pass the kitchen, then bedrooms, going farther and farther into the adult side. At the far end is the bathroom, tiled in salmon-pink tile, the seat in our minds of all the mysterious glamorous magic that goes on in this house. One half of it consists of the bathtub it-self, enormous, step-in, square and deep. All four of us can fit into it easily at once. On a counter below the mirror are perfume bottles of different shapes with different shades of gold liquid inside, Mary Chess ("French," our grand-mother says, her hand on the bottle, "very hard to find"), Opium, Chanel No. 5. To one side there's a bidet that intrigues us. Later, once our grandmother's gone, we'll play with it, spraying it up, the sudden flowering burst of cold between your legs. Along one wall hang lacy white nightgowns—dozens, it seems—soaked in perfume. Our grandmother puts the bathwater on and pours in bubble bath. She turns and picks out two of the nightgowns. "Here, gurls, these are for you."

*

Later, waterlogged after hours in the pool, another long hour in the bath, dizzy with the smell of our perfume-soaked nightgowns, our stomachs gorged with rich food, Lu and I lie in our twin beds with the engravings of white men chasing Indians hanging above us on the wall.

Our mother comes in in her dress with fringes. The lamp is out, but there's light coming through the doorway.

Chester has already gone to bed. In the background, out again by the pool, we can still hear Alec's voice: "You put the left-hand shot in the right-hand corner." Our mother sits down. She's about to say something, but then we hear our grandmother in the corridor.

"Faye, are you there?"

Our mother hesitates for a second. "Yeah, here, Mum."

Our grandmother appears in the bedroom doorway. "Oh," she says. She teeters there for a second, awkwardly, as if she might come in, but no one invites her. "Is everything okay?" she asks.

"Yeah, yeah, fine," our mother says.

"All right, then." Our grandmother, hesitating, turns away.

Our mother waits for a moment. Stiff, girl-like, in her Indian dress, she's sitting on the edge of my bed, but looking over at Lu, really talking to her. "She never not once tried to understand us," she says. "Why did she never once try to understand us?"

CREEPING

Our father goes around checking to make sure everything still works, things he's put in place himself, the plumbing—have the pipes frozen? The chimney—is it drawing well?

"Dad! Dad!" Lu and I yell, standing by the car. We know that our mother doesn't like him hanging around, and especially now that her boyfriend's so often here. It's winter. We're bundled up, Lu's breath white in the air. Tuck's still on the porch getting his boots on. Clyde puts his tongue against the frost-flowered car window.

"Awright, awright, awright!" our father says, skirting up the hill again, moving fast. He doesn't wear a full hat, just a band around his head that covers his ears. "Goddamned kids—they really keep you in line!"

The four of us pile into his low-slung brown car. As soon as we drive off, our father starts talking. It's always like this. It's as if he hasn't said a word since the last time we saw him. Does he talk to anyone besides us? We don't know. We can't imagine it.

"I was lying in bed the other day thinking about my life," he says. "And I realized that the one terrible thing, the only terrible thing that's ever happened to me is that I got divorced. Which meant that I didn't get to be with my kids. That has been the only terrible thing."

"But you do get to be with us," I say. I'm in the front, right where the heat pours out. I take off my coat, already feeling sweaty under my clothes.

"Yeah," Tuck says. He's leaning up between the seats.

"Yeah, yeah, I do, sort of, but not really. Not every day. It's a whole other thing to see a person every day."

But is our father all right? It seems like he's driving faster than usual. He's hunched down lower over the wheel.

"Dad, you're pulling down!" Clyde, the littlest, yells from the back.

He straightens. Out the windows, the same scenes whir by, the farmhouses, the dips in the road. We drive by our school on the other side of town, deserted now for the holidays—it's right after Christmas. We pass the orchards, black branches against the sky. Below, there's the pond where we go skating. We speed around a curve.

Our father is, as usual, telling us the news. It's always a combination of his ideas—always in the interval when we haven't seen him, he's come up with new ideas—things that happened, dreams he's had. He's all fired up about a project to design a new kind of brick stove. A Swedish guy has already attempted the thing. "Those Swedes," he says, "they're incredible, they're serious. Pick a Swede, any Swede, and he's sure to blow your mind."

He got a parking ticket and contested it and they didn't make him pay. "Those bastards actually read my little explanation and decided I didn't have to pay. Pretty good, eh? You're impressed, eh, Tuck? I may look dumb."

Clyde giggles. "You look funny with your hair like that."

We all look over at our father. He's taken off his ear band and his hair is now sticking out straight from his head. We laugh. Tuck reaches over the seat to pat it down.

"Thank you for sharing, Clyde," our father says.

He's just been to a high-security prison. He's teaching the inmates how to sing rounds. He had a dream about "Mom." He calls our mother "Mom." "It was amazing," he says. He leans back, one hand on his chest, eyes closed, to show how amazing it was. "She was something like twenty feet tall."

"Dad!" Lu says. There's a car coming toward us.

Our father opens his eyes, swerves to the right. "Oh, and the damnedest thing happened the other day— completely by accident, I picked up a whore!"

"A what?" Tuck asks.

"A whore! A prostitute!"

"What's that?" Tuck asks.

"Someone who has, you know, sex with you for money. I didn't mean to. There was just this woman standing there by the side of the road. I pulled over because I thought something was wrong. A redhead, nice-looking, in a green sort of coat. But without saying anything, she climbed right in and started telling me where to go. I still didn't get what the hell was going on. She must have thought I was retarded, it took me so long. But anyway, finally, I understood. And by then, well, it was too late. She took me to this place, this little room. And well, we did the thing, and it was fine, it was nice. But what was amazing to me was the way she cleaned herself afterward, so carefully by the little sink. That was the part about it that really blew my mind."

Lu's face is squinched up. She's in the back. "Did you pay her?" she asks.

"Yeah, yeah, I paid her. Of course I paid her. She was asking for fifty bucks, so I gave her sixty. Jesus, sixty. It was all I had."

We've made it to the highway. "Watch out, Dad, there's a cop!" Clyde says. Our father's always telling us to keep our eyes peeled for cops. There's one crouching in the center strip by the guardrail.

"Damn, you're right," he says. He slows way down.

*

The plan is to go skiing up north, staying at our grandmother's, but first we'll spend a night in the city. Our father wants to do what he calls a "big cleanup." His house is always a mess. He wants us to help him clean it. We've done this before.

We curve through the city, Washington, D.C., passing black and white monuments, lawns stiff with snow. Our father lives in a not-so-good neighborhood. The sidewalk is cracked up. Before, across the street was a drug den. Now it's boarded up. But people still linger out on the stoop. Sometimes when we're here, we play with the kids. Push is the girl's name, and the boy's called Big Daddy. Now when we pull up, Big Daddy is huddled on the stoop with some other kids. Big Daddy is older than Clyde but smaller.

"Big Daddy's smoking," Tuck says.

"Jesus Christ," our father says. He thinks that there's nothing in the world worse than smoking (though he used to smoke himself), except for maybe TV.

Our father's up on his stoop fiddling with the keys. "Awright, c'mon, you guys," he says.

We have to hurry when we're going into his house because there's an alarm. He's been robbed so many times he got an alarm. Even with the alarm though, he's still sometimes robbed. It's the power tools they're after. He has a lot of power tools because of his job, chimney repair.

Inside, his house is in shambles. It actually looks like someone's just been there to rob. There are papers piled everywhere, on the table and counters, the floor and the mantelpiece. On the couch is a pile of clothes, beside it a deposit of nails and string. The furniture, some of it inherited from his parents, our grandparents—an antique highboy, an ornately carved desk—is placed haphazardly, as if it's just been shoved in the door. Floating in the center of the room is a piano. Our father loves to sing, especially rounds. Sometimes he gets us to sing them with him, even though we usually screw things up. He cocks his ear hard, listening for the harmonies.

Our father leans over, rustling around in the refrigerator. "Time for some tofu eggs," he says. "Who's ready for tofu eggs? I can see Tuck's all fired up." Tuck, as we all know, doesn't like tofu.

We take off our coats and put down our bags. We're not sure where to sit because there's stuff all over everything.

"Damn!" our father says, noticing us lingering. He scurries over and clears off some chairs and a spot on the table.

I go look out at the backyard. "Dad," I say, "can I go out here?"

"Yeah, yeah," our father says. He's cooking the eggs. He fumbles in his shorts pocket for another key. He has a whole mass of them on a ring.

I unlock the door, first the one with the metal bars, then the other one, and step out. In the front half of the yard, there are a few drooping plants poking out of the snow. To the side, there's a high wall of wooden slats so you can't see the neighbor's yard.

I turn and look toward the back of the yard. It's another scene entirely, piled high with junk, an old milk truck, tiles, shingles and brick, blocks of wood and buckets, bags of sand and cement. I pick my way past the milk truck and through the junk pile. Closing in the backyard is a metal gate. Beyond it is the alley, the backs of everyone's houses, garbage cans, loose tires, and garbage on the ground. I imagine that it must be from this side that people come to steal. I'm looking and don't see anyone, and then suddenly I see a man crouched there, a young black guy. He's wearing a red down jacket. He's in the alley, crouched against the back gate of someone else's house. He doesn't make a move. He's staring back at me. I don't move, either. He must be one of the ones who come around to steal. I stay still for a moment, staring at him, paralyzed. Then a cat walks by and I move.

"Eggs!" our father calls. "Eggs are on!"

I turn and scurry back inside.

After lunch, we get to work cleaning. We know what to do. Tuck and Clyde are downstairs with our father, going through the piles of papers with him, some of our father's own writing, the rest newspapers, newsletters, bills, other mail. Tuck picks up each thing. He looks absurdly serious, his fat cheeks bright red. "This, Dad?"

"Naw, forget it," our father says. "We'll wait on that."

"No, Dad," Tuck insists. He's nine now. He knows how our father is. "Do you want to keep it or throw it away?"

Lu and I are in charge of the upstairs. I'm eleven, Lu's thirteen. One of the upstairs rooms is simply closed off, full of books and papers. The other two are bedrooms. We focus on these. On a table is a small shrine to our father's Hindu guru and all around it stacks of papers, files and clippings, ideas for articles, plans for solar energy projects. There are heaps of clothes and paintings tilted everywhere along the walls. Our father buys the paintings in thrift shops. The women in them always look just like our mother.

Lu starts in with the clothes. It's never quite clear if they're dirty or clean. She picks up each item, checks it, and makes a laundry pile and a clean, folded one. I begin to stack the paintings up neatly behind the bureau.

Our father is puttering around. Then he calls us from the bathroom at the end of the upstairs hall. He's already told us that he bought a new toilet. "Awright, you guys, c'mere! I want to show you how this baby works."

I look over at Lu. She rolls her eyes. The boys are stomping up the stairs. They get to the bathroom first.

Lu and I follow. We all gather around.

"Ewwww!" Clyde says, covering his nose at the smell. I've been holding my breath since long before I arrived. I can tell from Lu's face that she has been too.

"Tuck, hey, can you see?" our father asks.

"Yeah," Tuck says.

"Awright, look at this, it's amazing." There's a shit in the toilet bowl with very little water around it. The toilet itself looks funny. "It's one of those airplane things," he says. "It hardly uses any water. That's the whole point. A normal damn toilet just guzzles the stuff. Now watch." Our father flushes. There's a vacuum sucking sound, and the package that's there instantly disappears. He laughs. "Isn't that the damnedest thing?"

We all filter back to what we were doing.

A little while later, our father comes into the bedroom where Lu and I are. He looks around. "Damn, you guys, this is incredible! Jesus Christ!"

"We're just getting started, Dad," I say.

"No, no, that's enough for now."

He actually can't stand to clean up his house. It seems like any cleanup makes him nervous. He really wants to leave it just the way it is.

"C'mon, c'mon, c'mon," he says. "We gotta get out of here."

"Where are we going?" I ask.

"To Cindy's thingamajig."

Cindy's our father's present girlfriend. We've met her a few times.

"What thingamajig?" Lu says.

"I dunno. Some kind of thingamajig," our father says. He gets undressed and begins looking through the piles of clothes Lu has assembled. "Damn, where are those suckers?" he says.

"Dad, what do you need?" Lu says. He's standing there, no clothes on.

"The yellow suckers," he says. "Here they are!" He picks up a pair of yellow pants, puts them on, then his sandals over wool socks and a purple embroidered Indian shirt.

*

We clamber back into the car. Our father backs down the street the wrong way, then veers around.

"Where are we going?" Clyde asks.

"To Cindy's."

Clyde groans. "I thought we were going to the ashram!" Clyde loves our father's ashram, the big room with the red carpet and everyone chanting.

"Naw, another time," our father says.

Cindy lives in the suburbs. We pass empty lots with grill fences, people huddled on the sidewalk, shivering from the cold.

Clyde starts screaming the mantra they chant in the ashram: *"Om Namah Shivaya. OM NAMAH SHIVAYA!"*

"Clyde, shut up," Lu says.

"Cindy, geez. I haven't seen her in a while," our father says.

"Why?" I ask.

"I dunno. She was driving me crazy. She just talked all the time, talk, talk, talk. And especially after sex. That was when she talked the most. I mean, who the hell wants to talk after sex?"

Our father was with another woman for a while named Lonnie. They broke up about a year ago. Then he had a girlfriend who was completely different, a journalist. She had some kids and lived in a neighborhood full of trees. She would tease our father. Our father was going to ask her to marry him, but he asked our mother first if he should. Our mother said it wasn't any of her business. Our father didn't propose.

Cindy has short blond hair. She has a nice singing voice. She and our father sing together. But our father's always telling us things about Cindy that drive him nuts—her perfectly arranged house, her finicky hors d'oeuvres, her bright polite voice that cuts the air like glass. When we see her now, we look with that eye. It's all of us against her, judging her, chuckling.

Cindy's house is large and white with yellow trim, perched up on a piece of lawn. We've been here before out back for barbecues. But today cars line the street in front of it. Through the windows into the dining room, we see clusters of people standing around under the chandelier.

There's salt sprinkled over the icy walkway up to the front door. We follow our father, who's sidling slightly sideways. He rings the bell. Cindy opens the door. She looks our father up and down, and slams it closed again, leaving us outside. Our father laughs. After a moment,

Cindy opens the door again. She's dressed in a turquoise sweater dress, but has a coat on now. She steps out, closing the door quickly behind her.

"Sam!" she says. "Come here right now." She takes our father's hand and leads him down the stoop and around the side of the house. Our father shrugs and follows, wiggling his eyebrows. Cindy looks back at us, whispering loudly. "Come, come too!" We follow. "How could you do this?" she asks our father. She seems to be on the verge of tears. We're all out behind the house. "Okay," she says, collecting herself. "Now, I told everyone you were coming. My boss is here, my sister and her husband, old friends of Marty's and mine, so you have to come. But you can't wear those ridiculous clothes." She looks at us. "I told him exactly what to wear and I know he has the clothes because I've seen them in his closet, the khakis, the blue shirt." Our father's smiling. She turns back at him. She's obviously very angry. But then she composes herself, rubbing her hands together to stay warm. "Okay, I'm going to go upstairs and get you some of Marty's clothes. I'll throw them out the window and you can put them on in the car." She reaches up and presses our father's hair down with her hands. "And I'll throw out a comb too."

We wait with our father out behind the house. There's a layer of crunchy snow in Cindy's yard. Tuck kicks at it. He gets one piece free and kicks it across the surface so it sails. Clyde does the same.

"Is it a fancy party?" Lu asks.

We wish we were dressed up too. We wish he'd told us. Lu takes her hat off and pulls her fingers through her hair.

"We can use the comb," I say.

After ten minutes or so, the window opens above and Cindy's head appears. "Okay," she whispers. She drops down a bundle in a towel. Our father catches it. Cindy watches for a moment, then disappears. Our father unwraps the bundle. Inside, carefully folded, are khaki pants, a shirt with blue pinstripes, a navy blue V-neck sweater, lace-up shoes, thin dark socks, and a comb. Our father takes off his coat and then the rest of his clothes and changes right there outside in the cold. We look around to see if the neighbors are watching. The yards are all separated by fences, but if you look down from the upstairs windows, you can see everything. Someone has opened a window in the house across the alley and is shaking out a bedspread. First we see just the cloth shaking, then the woman's face. She stops and looks at us.

"Dad, hurry," I say, "someone's looking."

He's bent over, pulling the khakis on. He doesn't seem to care. At least, I think, she can only see his butt.

Lu combs her hair and hands the comb to me.

Our father stands up straight. "Damn, these shoes feel awful!" he says, shifting back and forth, wincing.

He puts his coat back on, bunches up his other clothes and scuttles off to hide them in the car.

A moment later, we're all once again on Cindy's door-step, only our father looks completely different now. The new clothes are slightly bulky in funny places, but they do the trick.

Cindy opens the door. "Hello," she says, acting, scrutinizing our father quickly, but deciding it's okay. She smiles her bright polite smile. "Come in, everyone's here."

Cindy's house is full of people. There's a punch bowl in the dining room and a fire going. With a few exceptions, people are dressed much more like our father is now. Cindy is a lawyer. Many of the guests are the people from her firm.

There's a den off the kitchen. Cindy says we kids can go in there if we like. She's gotten out some toys for us. Cindy never had children. Lu and I look down at the toys. We can't believe it. There are Legos, for example. In the room, there are also beanbag chairs. Tuck and Clyde pretend they're bulls and charge headlong into the beanbag chairs. Lu and I wander back into the party. There's music playing. A woman wearing boots has flung one leg over the arm of a chair as she talks to a guy. Cindy's moving around the room. She has her hand on our father's arm, introducing him to everyone.

We go back to the den. After a little while, we wander out, bored again. Our father's talking animatedly to someone across the room. It's one of Cindy's colleagues, a man in a suit. Cindy's watching from a slight distance. Then she steps nearer. She seems somewhat perturbed. She moves quickly over to them. She has her smile. She takes our father's arm. We can imagine what she's saying. "Can I steal him for a second?" She leads him with her into the kitchen, smiling brightly the whole way. The kitchen is at the end of a short hall. Lu and I edge near so we can hear.

"Do you have any idea who that was?" Cindy asks. "That's not my boss. It's my boss's boss. How could you have been telling him that?"

"Hey, c'mon—" our father says. But it seems like he actually really likes to get in trouble.

Cindy interrupts. "You know what it all boils down to? You have a boundary problem. I was talking to my shrink and I think you have a boundary problem. You don't know where your boundaries are."

"But listen, I was telling him about an experience I had."

"You were telling him about the shits you had."

Lu and I giggle. Our father must have been telling about the grape fast he did in the fall, eating only grapes for six weeks, which made him have all kinds of weird shits, first one kind, then another. We've heard the story a million times.

"Well, those were experiences," our father says.

"You know what? I think you should leave. I think you should really just leave now."

"Boundary problem?" our father says, once we're back in the car, pulling away from Cindy's. "Do you guys think I have a boundary problem?"

I'm not sure what he means. In any case, I shake my head, not wanting to agree with Cindy.

"What's a boundary problem?" Clyde asks.

"Exactly!" our father says. "Well put, Clyde!"

Our father's silent for a moment. Then he holds up a finger. "You know what I think the problem is?" he says. "I think the problem, her whole problem, is that she's never had such good sex in her life."

*

Next morning, we're on the road again, heading north, our skis hooked to the roof. We've been going skiing with our father since we were born. On the slopes, we do relay races and play Follow the Leader. We duck down and go through each other's legs. It's a family rule to wear leather ski boots and never use poles. When we get stuck on the ski lift with a stranger, it's always the same.

"Nice gear you got there."

But first we have the drive. Our father's talking. "I've been going out with a lot of dogs recently," he says.

"Who was a dog?" I ask.

"All of them! Everyone. Cindy's pretty much of a dog. Even Lonnie."

"Lonnie?" we say. It's weird because they all seemed very pretty to us, especially Lonnie, even if we didn't like them in other ways.

"Who's *not* a dog, then?" Lu asks.

"Good question. Well, let's see, your Mom, for instance, could never be called a dog."

We pass roadside developments, frozen lakes, and farms. Sheer rock cliffs rise up along the side of the highway with rivulets of ice in the cracks. Sometimes there are signs that say FALLING ROCKS. But how would a Falling Rocks sign help you if there were rocks actually falling? We go under a bridge with the words *I Love You Tony* spray-painted across the top. We stop at gas stations. Lu always goes to the bathroom and comes back with her hair wet and flattened. Once we drive off with the hose from the gas pump still in our tank. The attendant, in a red and yellow uniform, comes running out after us.

"Hey, what the hell are you doing?"

As the light's fading, we see signs for Boston. "You know what we're going to do?" our father says. "We're going to nip in and see if we can stay with old George. You guys remember George, right?"

"Yeah," I say. Our father went to college with George. We stopped here once with Lonnie.

"And his wife—"

"The professor," I say.

"That's right, the professor. Damn, Maeve, good for you!"

Dusk is falling as we enter the city. We see stone buildings with domes. We circle a hill. By the Boston Common, we pass a guy with a truck and a loudspeaker. There are stickers all over the truck, antinuclear, anti-Reagan. The guy has fingerless gloves on. He's all bundled up and speaking into the loudspeaker.

"Damn," our father says, "goddamn hippies, still at it!" He slows down, creeping by, so he can look at the guy. "I mean, Jesus Christ," he says, "take a look at this guy. Who the hell's listening to him?" He drives on. "Though, okay, I admit, there were some guys, a few guys, who got themselves out there. Though few, very few, given all the bastards who tried. And we're talking about smart bastards, I mean really smart bastards. I bet that bastard is really smart."

It's dark by the time we find the house. We remember it, a brownstone in a street of brownstones with a dark blue door and a knocker. It seems very quiet. We knock. No one answers at first. Finally, George's wife, Pat, opens the door.

"Hey," our father says. "All right, you're here!"

Slim with short dark hair, she's in pajamas and a robe. The house is dark behind her. It's clear she doesn't want to see us. "But George isn't," she says. "He's gone off with the kids."

"Oh, well . . ." Our father shifts his weight.

She shivers a bit because of the cold air coming in. "I needed to be alone to finish a book," she says.

"A book!" our father says. "Damn! Good for you."

We're standing on the stoop, our backpacks on our shoulders. Pat doesn't say anything.

"Dad." Lu pulls on his shirt and whispers, "Let's go."

But our father barrels ahead. It's the way he gets when he's talking to our mother, asking her for something he knows she doesn't want to give. He's hunched down, neck jutting out, one hand wagging, both leaning forward and backing away. "Would it be all right if we came inside?"

Pat lets out her laugh like a bark. "Well, if you put it that way," she says. Her voice sounds hoarse. She steps back, no longer blocking the door.

But now we kids really don't want to go in.

"C'mon, c'mon, c'mon," our father says, herding us through the door.

Pat leads us down a hallway into the living room. It's dark and chilly, as if no one's been in there for a while or the shutters are all closed. There's heavy wood paneling on the walls.

"What's the book about?" our father asks.

"The origins of war," Pat says.

"Shit! Damn," our father says. "The origins of war."

Pat looks at him, one eyebrow raised.

"You know there was a guy," our father says, "interesting bastard, E-Ed-Ed-Edgars was his name. Do you know him? He was at Harvard when George and I were there. He was working in the same line, I think, blood rites, primitive warfare. I could track him down for you, though, shit, it's been a while. Except for George I haven't seen those guys for tw-tw-twenty-some years."

"I have all the reference material I could possibly use," Pat says. "But I need to go on working, so let's get straight to the point. You want to stay here for the night." Her look is deadpan. She states it as a fact. The last time we came we also stayed for the night.

Our father adopts his squeamish pose again, hunched, head bobbing. "That would be great," he says.

"Okay," Pat answers, already leaving the room. "You can help yourselves to whatever you want in the kitchen.

I don't know what there is. I'm not even going to look. The guest room's back there. I'll throw down some sleeping bags."

"Great, great," our father repeats, rubbing his hands, following Pat, who's already climbing back up the stairs.

We leave our backpacks in the guest room and go into the kitchen.

"Dad," Lu whispers, "she doesn't want us here!"

"Naw, naw, it's all right. It's good for her. Builds character."

He rummages through the cupboards and finds what he needs to make tuna fish spaghetti. He turns to us, speaking softly. "Now, speaking of dogs, *she* is not a dog."

We look at him. We can't believe it.

"Pat?" I ask.

"You think she's pretty?" Lu asks.

She seems so hard and stiff and cold.

Tuck pulls out the playing cards.

Seeing them, Clyde jumps up. "Hey, Dad," he says, "can we play bridge?"

"Yeah, yeah," our father says, "let's play some bridge." He taught us how. Since then, we always play bridge when we're with him. Now the four of us play a hand while our father cooks.

When the spaghetti's ready, our father fills our plates, then one for himself and another. He walks out of the kitchen with the last plate.

"Dad, where are you going?" Lu asks, vigilant.

"I'm gonna see if Pat wants some."

I can see him through the doorway from where I'm sitting. He slinks up the stairs.

"C'mon, let's play!" Clyde yells.

"Shh," Lu says. She and I both want and don't want to hear what's happening.

We hear our father's voice, mild, soft: "Pat, Pat."

A door opens. We can picture our father's posture, the same as before, hunched down, wobbling, holding out the plate but backing away.

"No, no, thanks," Pat says. The door closes again.

Our father comes back downstairs with the full plate. He shrugs and laughs. "She's a toughie," he says.

It's the middle of the night. Lu and I are in the guest bed, our father and the boys in sleeping bags on the floor. I wake and see our father getting up quietly. He's naked.

He slips out of the room, but instead of going in the direction of the bathroom, he goes the other way. He's creeping up the stairs. Oh no, what's he doing? I sit up, then get up. There's silence. I go out of the room and stand near the stairs. I hear footsteps creeping, the soft sound of a door. Then a surprised muffled shout, Pat, and furious whispering. Our father, lingering slightly, makes a shuffling retreat as the furious whispering grows louder.

I dash back to the room. Our father comes down again. Out the window now, there's the first light in the sky.

"Okay, kids," our father says, whispering, waking us. "C'mon, c'mon, c'mon, let's get outta here."

Lu wakes and looks at him with one eye. "Why?"

"We gotta get an early start," he says.

The other three are grumpy. But I, like my father, want to get the hell out of there.

We get dressed, shove our stuff into our backpacks, roll the sleeping bags up again, and straighten the bed. All around us the house is quiet and dark and cool. We tiptoe down the hallway, open the door and creep with our father out into the dawn.

SECRET

It was through our friend Shirley that we met the Kalowski boys. I was twelve that summer and my sister, Lu, was fourteen. (Our brothers, younger, were at that time in our lives peripheral figures.) Shirley used to live in the hollow down below us but had recently moved up the road, where the houses were more populous, closer to the hard road and the still faraway town. For years, in our little enclave in the woods, Shirley had lorded over my sister and me and our other friend, Trish, who lived over the hill.

Shirley was my sister's age. She didn't have a father. She had sandy hair and small eyes that almost closed up when she smiled. She had a rich fantasy life to which we were all meant to adhere. All games, as long as we remembered, had been under her dominion, in the pasture, on the ponies, lounging on the creek bank in the sun: "Okay, I'm the empress, you're the lady-in-waiting, you're the messenger." "Okay, I'm the prettiest, you're the second prettiest." Lu had spaces between her teeth and always carried her head tilted to one side. I thought she was the prettiest. But it didn't matter what we thought. Shirley was in charge.

She staged her dark dream life with us as actors. Death was everywhere. She taught us how to make each other faint. One person leans over and hyperventilates, while the other grips her from behind and holds tight across her diaphragm, then drops her in the pasture grass out cold. You'd come to, head spinning, thinking hours had passed. Shirley was obsessed at different times with the Manson murderers—"They kill you, whole families, and hang your bodies on the clothesline"—whom she assured us would soon be coming here, and Henry VIII and his wives. Another game was to have one of us go into a dark closet and turn around eight times saying "Mary Walker." It didn't always work but it could happen sometimes that the ghost of Mary Walker would come out and kill you.

I can see Shirley singing Donna Summer—*"Toot, toot, yeah, beep, beep"*—and swirling her hip. Standing by the mailbox of her new house along the road, still a dirt road but wider and more trafficked than the tiny path that trickled by our house, and waiting for the chance to catch someone's eye. She flourished in this new environment, where there were people driving by, eyes to catch, and she soon got to know all the neighborhood characters—Michael Melton, Bonnie Rider, Marcy, the Lyalls. My sister and I were now like the country cousins, while Shirley had been out and seen the world. She'd ride her pony over to our house to give a report, delighting in the ambassadorial role.

Michael Melton's father sat on the porch of their low ranch house drinking all day with a gun in his hands and shot at things that passed by on the road—squirrels, stray dogs, cars. Michael's mother dressed herself and Michael's sister, Mindy, exactly the same, in skirts or patterned pants suits, like two dolls. Michael was older than Mindy, fourteen or so, very tall, with gray teeth. He was an amazing athlete and his name was familiar to Lu and me since we'd heard it mentioned over the loudspeaker for winning sports prizes at school.

Bonnie Rider was adopted. She had a pale, grave, watchful face and gray-brown hair. Behind her house was a pond full of weeds. Bonnie was friends with Marcy. "Marcy's cool," Shirley said offhandedly, as if she and Marcy were now very close. Lu and I knew enough who Marcy was—the coolest girl in school—to know this couldn't be true. But we were used to Shirley's lies. She lied about everything.

The Lyalls had a blue plastic out-of-ground swimming pool. Everyone spent as much time at their house as possible. They kept a cooler full of sodas in the dark garage. All the Lyalls had Renaissance faces, dark shoulder-length hair that curled at the ends, along their temples or lower cheeks, and clear, soft features. They were slim and retiring in manner and had a yard full of trash and flower bushes right at the corner where the bus stop was.

But the big news that summer was the arrival of the Kalowski boys, two brothers from the city. Their parents took the farm up the road from Shirley's. There were rumors that they'd moved because there'd been trouble in the city, nobody knew exactly what. The Kalowski boys wore city clothes and smoked cigarettes. They were thirteen and fourteen. They were soon tight with Michael Melton, friends with Tim Lyall. This whole business of country life was strange to them—their farm had come with two ponies and a cow—but the boys took it in stride, flipping their legs over the ponies as if they were motorbikes, congregating in the woods instead of on street corners, thinking up new ways to vandalize.

Shirley had gone out riding with them more than once. An expert herself on all things "equestrian" (that was the word she liked to use), she said that their ponies were much too small for them and, besides that, they didn't know how to ride. When she'd tried to give them pointers, they wouldn't listen. They'd veer off instead to spray paint a driveway or topple the statues on Ed Trout's pristine lawn. Shirley had told the boys about my sister and me and they were eager to meet us, not so much for the reason she'd thought, because we had ponies too, but because they'd heard from Tim Lyall that our mother and her boyfriend were hippies and would go swimming naked at our swimming hole.

One day, Shirley arranged for us all to meet up on ponies outside her house.

Shirley made the introductions. "Lu's my age," she explained, "but four months younger. Trish and Maeve are both eleven, but Maeve's younger by a month and a half." (As usual, I was always less or the least.)

The older boy, Sid, was wiry, with chicken-like arms and legs and one dark tooth on the side. His legs dangled off his tiny pony. He couldn't stop jittering.

"You know, in the future human beings won't have bodies anymore," he said.

"Why?" Shirley said.

"Because they won't need them. They hardly need them now. Most everything they can do with their minds."

The younger one, Jesse, had an angelic face and a small paunch, his blond hair curling in his eyes and ears. "You know, our brother, Lee, lives on a nuclear submarine."

"Why?" Trish asked. While Lu and I looked at the boys without really looking—Lu took her ponytail out and put it in again; I pretended to scratch my insect bites—Trish looked directly. She had a pointed nose and thin, sleek hair. She stared at the boys' mouths, not their eyes, her own lips parted somewhat. When she acted like this, I thought she was dumb, but later I realized there were other reasons.

Jesse noticed her looking at him and looked back, languorously, rubbing his stomach with one hand. "Because he's in the army," he said. "There's a war on with the Russians. Didn't you know?" Suddenly, his face lit up. "Oh, shit, Sid, there he is!"

Ed Trout's white pickup truck had appeared coming slowly down the road. "Let's go, go, go!" Jesse said. He kicked his pony hard. The pony, taken by surprise, shot out across the road and plunged straight into the field of wheat on the other side. Jesse slipped to one side, pulled himself up, then slipped to the other, clinging to his pony's neck. Sid followed Jesse. I saw a stroke of confusion, then elation, cross Lu's face. She kicked her pony. I kicked mine. We all plunged after the boys into the wheat, cutting pathways, running blindly.

When we came out again, over by the Ballards' farm, I looked over my shoulder. You could see in the distance the white pickup coming after us. My heart was racing.

"This way!" Sid said.

We galloped down the road, then ducked into the woods behind the Lyalls' house. We waited there, panting, hiding. The smell of a lilac bush was very strong. Off to one side were the ruins of an old house. A rusted metal bedstead still stood in one of the rooms.

We heard the pickup pass by. A moment later, it turned and came back the same way, then the sound of it grew fainter and fainter. We waited until the sound had disappeared altogether and then walked out through the trees until we got to the Lyalls' yard.

We tied our ponies up in the Lyalls' yard on the little straggly trees beside the mounds of trash with enough rein so they could eat grass. The grass was very lush, maybe from garbage. There was already a crowd. Michael Melton, his toes gripping the thin metal edge of the pool, did swan dives—you could see the hair in his armpits as he lifted his arms—or cannonballs. The whole point was to hit someone. He'd aim right for your head.

We all got in the pool. Shirley didn't have her bathing suit on so she climbed in in her clothes. She tried to organize one of her games, this one about King Arthur and the Knights of the Round Table—she would play Guinevere—but no one listened. Not even Trish and I, the little ones, listened. The truth was we were pretty sick of listening to her, and now, besides, there was so much else to see. Only Tim Lyall listened, very politely, his clear Renaissance face never swerving from hers. He seemed to listen to anyone who spoke forcefully and with conviction, and had, it seemed, maybe precisely for this reason, a particular crush on Shirley. She soon settled down to just addressing him. They edged over to the side of the pool.

Marcy came by. She wore tight blue jeans, though it was summer, and a see-through shirt with silver thread in it. She was thirteen, same as Lu. She leaned her elbows up against the pool and asked Sid if he had cigarettes. Shivering, blue, he climbed up out of the water, more than happy to oblige. Marcy's hair, the glossiest blue-black I'd ever seen, was shoulder length, swept back in feathers. She wasn't getting wet. She'd be in eighth grade next year. Her bra showed through her shirt—we all looked at it. She wandered off again, a vacant look on her face, completely conscious of the effect she made, and went to talk to Denise Lyall, who was even older than Marcy but had been held back a year, and was sitting inside with a perm in her hair. A little bit later, Bonnie Rider came by. She stared into the pool for a few minutes, saying nothing, her grave, motionless face showing just above the edge, then she, too, went into the house.

As far as swimming went, it was much more satisfying to be in the creek. Here in this plastic-cubicle world there was no space whatever to move around. The water was stagnant and full of human fluids. You could be hit at any moment by a human cannonball. But the scene was riveting to watch. I could see Lu watching, pressed against the edge, head tilted to the side, a strand of hair caught in her mouth.

That night Lu and I lay awake, picturing Marcy's bra through her shirt, Sid's one dark tooth, Ed Trout coming after us, our hearts pounding with excitement.

From then on, we went out riding with the boys nearly every day. Sometimes we went by their house to pick them up. Their yard was always quiet. There was a rose of Sharon bush, a clothesline, upturned cars, a few dark kittens here and there. Their father, a mechanic with a blond cowlick, would peer out from behind one of the cars. Their mother was nearly always inside. She had an angelic face, like Jesse's, hair wrecked by treatments. Inside, the house was dark and filled with stuffed sofas and chairs. Their mother spent most of her time sitting on the couch with her eight-year-old daughter, watching TV. Like the father, she was very young. They slept upstairs in a large heart-shaped bed. When a neighbor came by to complain about the boys, their father would hide behind the hood of one of his cars. Their mother would come out of the house and listen, nodding, perplexed, like a little girl, then go back inside. There was a photo of the older brother propped up on the TV.

Or the boys came to our house. Although our father had moved out a while ago and our house had changed a lot since—an addition had been built; there were now rooms and doors—it still had the reputation of being a hippie house, or so Shirley had told us, with rumors circulating about walls painted all sorts of funny colors, and weird experiments and wild parties going on. The first time the Kalowski boys came over, they couldn't but be disappointed. The walls were wood-colored and there was no one around. But there were a few things to marvel at all the same: the swing hanging from the center of the ceiling—Lu got up on it and did all the tricks she knew—and the paintings of naked people done by a friend of our mother's. The boys went over and stood in front of the naked paintings, whispering and jabbing each other with their elbows. They were very eager to see our mother swimming naked, as Tim Lyall had. What they didn't know was that our mother had changed too. Although she still went swimming naked, and had spent a night in jail not long ago for protesting at a nuclear plant, she'd also recently done a stint as head of the PTA. The boys hung around waiting for her to appear and, when she did, looked her up and down. Since it was summer, and she was mostly in the garden, she had bare feet and wore cutoff shorts. Lu and I knew what they were thinking.

We took them down to the swimming hole, where we plunged right in, still on our ponies' backs, hot and sticky, without even taking off our clothes. The ponies wobbled at first, hoofs sinking into the mud, then, necks long, heads pulsing forward, began to swim. I gripped my pony's back with my legs. The water made everything feel different. Lu let her legs free so they streamed out behind her, just clinging with both hands to her pony's mane.

The boys came out of the water. Sid was shivering. He had a little sneer whenever he was wet and partially dressed, as if he were frightened or disgusted by his body. "Did you see the movie *2001: A Space Odyssey*?" he asked.

Lu and I shook our heads.

"Me neither. But there's a computer in there that tries to take over from humans."

Jesse, fresh, white-skinned, went to scratch his back on a nearby tree.

Our parents' figures faded. I could see it on my sister's face. We were no longer thinking so much about them, our father's feeling abandoned, our mother's new boyfriend. And we weren't worrying, either, about the other things we worried about, school next year. Our minds were elsewhere, out riding with the boys, tearing through the trees. The creek water clung to our skin, hair, clothes. We dove headlong into the world and then back headlong into bed. We woke smelling of creek water or pool water and ponies.

Soon Trish wasn't allowed to play with us and the Kalowski boys. They were "bad boys," her parents said. Their older brother, Lee, was in jail. Now she sat alone in her house, watching out the windows. It was a charity gesture to go and see her when we could be having so much fun.

The boys lied. They told stories about their brother. ("The submarine he's on has made it over to Russia now," Jesse said. "They're spying off the coast.") Shirley lied. The lies gave a surreal quality to the world.

I had the first little nubs of breasts. Lu, older by two years, had nothing. Shirley had actual boobs. When she had first started to get them, too soon, Lu had been delighted still to be flat. "You'll be sorry later," Shirley had said. Now Lu was. I heard the boys walking behind us one day and whispering about our breasts. I saw them staring at our shirts. They were curious and least shy around Shirley. Once they took her aside and questioned her, a conversation that she reported afterward:

"Does Lu have hair down there?"

"No."

"Does Maeve?"

"No."

"Do you?"

"She told them she did."

We were curious about them too. We could see through their shorts when they had an erection. Sid's voice was changing. He had some hair in his armpits.

The boys bragged about this or that, but nothing happened. Not yet. At the Lyalls' pool, everyone was squirming, jittering, pushing the envelope. Shirley was part of this, too. My sister and I watched. We knew quite a bit about adult sex from seeing our parents' friends frolic at parties. We were a little bit behind, and at the same time far ahead. What had been forbidden to them hadn't been forbidden to us. We'd seen more grown-ups swimming naked than we cared to think about. What we hadn't seen, though, were things like Michael Melton's dad, red-eyed, hurling insults, firing a shotgun blindly from his porch at the road. The boys said that Michael Melton came over to their house at night and had sex with their ponies, surely another lie. We hadn't been exposed to violence or cruelty of that kind, the way, for example, Michael Melton would hurl a kitten hard against a tree, breaking its skull.

When my pony got hurt one day, I rode along behind Sid on his, leg to leg, my arms around his bony chest. I could have felt a lot of things, like laying my head down on his back, the hot thin T-shirt against my face.

The summer sky spiraled upward. It cast a fantasy light over the wheat, the pasture grass, and the trees. Lu and I lay awake, hearts pounding. The world was different now. We were thinking about other things: the future, outer space, not our parents, not Shirley and her hierarchical games.

We'd go riding in the pouring rain, under lightning. Or we'd wait it out awhile under the trees. Sid, skin and bones, was shivering, his face blue. My sister lay back along the spine of her horse. Her yellow shirt clung to her skin. The trees sheltered us almost completely from the rain. A roll of thunder crossed the sky. Then lightning. Lu sat up.

✳

That year, when school began, things were different too. We were all by now in the middle school. While our elementary school had been a small pink building with rows of trees and a playground outside, the middle school, in contrast, was huge and angular, built from cinder blocks, with almost no windows. Instead of a playground, there was a vast indoor gym. All the elementary schools in the area, including ours, fed into the middle school. In the broad concrete hallways, the fluorescent lights blared down. Crowds accumulated. There were far too few teachers to control all the kids. The principal seemed to relish all the paddling he did.

For the Kalowski boys, school provided a whole new set of opportunities to misbehave. Although they started out in the sixth and eighth grades, they were soon put into the "retarded" class, a class for both the mentally retarded and simply very bad. The boys and their friends from the retarded class traveled the hallways in a marauding horde, throwing things, shouting, knocking on doors as they went by. Lu and I were in the "gifted and talented group." The boys' friends would make comments about us. They would grab us between the legs as we passed by in the halls. The Kalowski boys wouldn't dare do these things themselves, but we couldn't help wondering if they weren't directing operations. One friend of theirs in particular, Marshall, always grabbed me between the legs. I would turn my back to the wall and slide along it whenever I saw him coming my way.

Sid stole things: jackknives or hats from kids' lockers, science magazines from the library. He was so skinny he could slip the magazines down the back of his pants. Jesse was more flamboyantly bad. He'd pinch the social studies

teacher's butt—Miss Dandy had lovely, large curves everywhere, including her butt, and a limp because of one leg
that dragged—or pick a fight with another kid in the gym.
As he was hauled off to the principal's office, he had his
usual look of fear mixed with delight. The boys were kept
in for detention all the time. They were paddled. The principal, Mr. Loehmann, was a medium-sized man with wire-
framed glasses and teeth with jagged edges. He wore shirts
with small colored stripes. His rounded shoulders were too
large for the rest of his body. He must have had, or at least
acquired, strength from all the paddling he did.

At the end of the school day, the yellow round-nosed
buses lined up in front of the school. The Kalowski boys
would come to the bus after having been paddled, holding
their butts in their hands. One day, when the long line of
buses was just beginning to move, Marcy stood up and
yelled, "Wait!" We looked over and saw Jesse running out
of the front door of the school with the principal, Mr.
Loehmann, on his tail. Jesse ran for the bus, the principal
right behind him. The bus driver, Mr. Hershey—a red-
haired man with a beard who every few minutes along the
road to and from school looked up into the large tilted mirror above his head and yelled, "Keep it down!" or "In your

seats!"—waited just a second longer as Jesse neared and opened the door. Jesse leapt on, Mr. Hershey closed the door, and the bus pulled away, leaving Mr. Loehmann out on the pavement. Everyone went berserk. Mr. Hershey pretended not to understand anything, but a moment later as we turned out the school driveway, Trish and I saw him smile.

The bus was a world unto itself. It was like being in a room where everything was too loud, music playing, people yelling, the TV on, and then outside the silent land-scape streaming by: wheat fields, cornfields, farms, and clumps of trees. Everyone was squirming, straining, either to hide away or make themselves heard. The windows fogged over with breath and sweat. Jesse snapped Marcy's bra strap. Michael Melton hulked down the aisle to grab the retarded boy. Shirley was telling Bonnie Rider about past lives, turned around in her seat, propped up on one knee, screaming above the noise. Sometimes one or another of the bad boys peed and, depending on whether we were go-ing up or down a hill, the pee would run forward or back along the aisle.

It was a relief to step off the bus out into the air, which felt cool and clear, late fall now, though your ears were still ringing. The Lyalls and the Meltons scattered to their houses. Trish's parents were waiting to pick her up. Marcy and Bonnie Rider walked a ways with us.

Shirley went on with what she was saying. "I was Queen Elizabeth the First."

"But how do you know?" Bonnie asked.

Lu was walking beside them, carrying her violin. The days were getting shorter, the pink-yellow light of sundown already in the air.

"You just know."

"And so that means in the next life you'll be someone else?" Bonnie asked.

"Yeah, sure," Shirley said.

"You'll definitely come back and be someone else with a different life?"

Shirley shrugged, delighted to have Bonnie Rider hanging on her every word. "Of course."

Sid came up beside me. He had a science magazine tucked into the back of his pants. "You know a nuclear war would mean the end of the world," he said. "Everything, the whole planet, would be destroyed."

Marcy was eyeing Jesse. She was about a head taller, walking beside him. "Hey, do you have a cigarette?" she asked.

Jesse dug into his pocket and pulled out a bent cigarette. He found some matches and lit it for her. He watched Marcy lean down, her face near his hands.

"You know, our brother, Lee, was captured by the Russians," he said. He put his hand inside his jacket to touch his stomach.

Marcy inhaled. She flipped her hair coolly. "What do they want from him?" she asked.

"They're trying to get him to tell nuclear secrets."

"Really? Does he know nuclear secrets?"

"Of course! He knows everything."

We still went riding sometimes on the weekends, but it had grown cold and Lu and I had other things to do, like homework.

Sid and Jesse never did their homework and didn't even always go to school. One day, Jesse's mother promised him twenty dollars if he got an A on a test. He asked Lu and me if we could help him. It was a geography test and he had to memorize the continents and oceans on the globe. He came over to our house to study and was distracted only momentarily by the sight of our mother. The following day, he came home from school holding the test paper high in his hand. He'd gotten an A. His mother was beaming. Jesse clearly could have gone on like this, with just minimal studying, and done well. But this wasn't what interested him. The rewards elsewhere were more gratifying. He had it in his blood, the thrill of being bad, much more intoxicating than any A.

Lu and I went about our school days. To combat any weird rumors about our house, we tried to act as normal as we could. We carried combs in our back pockets, flipped our hair back, trying to imitate the cooler girls. The rewards for us were in getting A's. We got A's. But we were also torn about it. We had always been debilitated by this penchant of ours to get A's, because getting A's wasn't cool. We tried to stop but couldn't. We were caught in a bind. We walked around with our friends. In the halls, we ducked to avoid being thrown against the lockers by a teacher, too enraged and helpless to see whom he was hitting. We skirted along against the wall to avoid having our pussies grabbed by Sid and Jesse's friends. We played instruments in the orchestra, my sister the violin, me the cello. My sister changed her part to the middle—mine was still on the side—and soon afterward became a cheerleader, an enormous step toward being cool. I went on getting A's, debilitating myself.

Shirley was not that cool, either, but her big boobs helped her a lot in other ways. She and Lu were still friends. They walked around carrying their books up near their chests. But Lu had other friends, too, especially now that she was a cheerleader, and Shirley had found other acolytes to listen to her. She could always find acolytes to listen to her. Trish, twelve now like me, who hadn't been able to ride with us and the Kalowski boys because her parents were terrified she'd get pregnant young, had suddenly out of nowhere begun making out with boys between the lockers. Though she was pretty occupied with this, we were still friends.

Lu and I were still friends with the Kalowski boys, though it was a strange sort of communication—as if we were spies meeting on the border of foreign territories, speaking in code. We'd exchange confidences in the hall. Lu and I both at different times covered for them. Once Sid came speeding by me and passed off a jackknife, which I didn't know what to do with and stuffed into the front pocket of my jeans. He was being chased. All day, the jackknife stayed there, pressing against my thigh.

Another time, in the hall, Lu lied for Jesse, saying she'd seen him go one way when he'd gone the other. A few minutes later, as Lu was walking down the hall talking to her cheerleader friend, the science teacher, Miss Lehr, who had a rough manner and a boxy face, grabbed Lu from behind by the hair.

"You know what that's called?" she said, bringing her large square head close to Lu's. She had a scratchy, sensual voice. "Aiding and abetting." She still had Lu's head yanked back, Lu's neck exposed. She seemed to be relishing this, and to want to keep Lu in this position for as long as she could. That day, after school, Lu, her face burning and the roots of her hair still sore, had to stay for detention.

I would sometimes run into Marcy, usually in the bathroom. She'd be looking in the mirror putting eyeliner on—she wore it very dark along the lower lid—and singing softly to herself, *"Welcome to the Hotel California..."* Once I was in a stall when she and Denise Lyall and Bonnie Rider came in. They were loud, in a mood. Or at least Denise and Marcy were. Marcy had colored pieces of chalk, probably stolen from the science room. I was in a stall peering out. They were talking about boys. Bonnie wrote *Fuck* with the chalk in big letters on the wall. For some reason, I felt scared and stayed where I was in the stall. Denise was giggling a lot. Bonnie watched. She smiled. She seemed to have a secret.

Then something wonderful happened. Marcy decided that she wanted to "go with" Jesse, even though he was younger than her and in the retarded class. She had the message conveyed to him by Denise.

Jesse's delight was immeasurable. Now Marcy walked down the hall with him, his hand on her butt. They sat together on the bus. It was clear from Jesse's expression, sitting there, his arm hooked around her shoulder, that he couldn't believe his luck and none of the rest of us could, either. Denise and Bonnie Rider sat in the seat in front of them so the three girls could still talk. Denise tried to flirt with Sid, but it didn't work. He was too shy. Bonnie Rider watched gravely. Once off the bus, Jesse and Marcy went into the woods behind the Lyalls' to do things on the abandoned bed out there. They'd hauled out a foam mattress and a stash of blankets, Tim Lyall said. But they also couldn't wait. They did things at school. Marcy would wear no underwear if he asked her. She'd let him unhook her bra behind the gym. Once I passed them making out between the lockers and heard Marcy moan. For a long time I couldn't get that sound out of my head.

One day when we were walking home from the bus stop, after Marcy and Jesse had slipped off into the woods, Sid came up to me. Lu and Shirley were walking ahead. He was jittery, glancing around as if he was afraid of something.

"I could kiss you," he said.

I looked at him, too surprised even to blush. He moved off, a science magazine tucked into the back of his pants.

After that, he came up to me every once in a while, passing by me in the hall at school or on the way home from the bus stop, and said very softly so no one could hear, "I'll kiss you soon."

At first, when he said it, I felt confused. I wasn't actually sure if I wanted to kiss him or anyone at all. When I saw my friend kissing boys between the lockers, her cheeks long and contorted, it didn't look like something I wanted to do. But even though I wasn't sure I wanted to kiss Sid, I began to look forward to him saying that to me. He said it like a threat, but it wasn't threatening. And the more he said it and didn't do anything, the more curious I got.

Once, on the walk home from the bus stop, he grabbed my wrist and whispered it, his lip grazing my ear. I turned my face to his, but he quickly moved off again.

Finally, I couldn't stand it anymore, and one day, a Saturday in early spring, I went down to the pasture to get my pony and, without telling anyone, rode up the road alone.

I took the back way so as to avoid passing in front of Shirley's house. Though the ground was still frozen, there were the first green buds on the trees.

The Kalowski boys' yard, as usual, was still. I rang the bell. Their mother came out, her hair wrapped in blue plastic.

"Is Sid here?" I asked.

She called up to him. He answered. Jesse, as I figured, wasn't around, off somewhere with Marcy.

"One of the girls is here to see you."

Sid appeared on the stairs. He saw me and immediately looked scared, as if he knew what I'd come for. He ducked his face. "I'll be right there," he said, and went back upstairs.

But he didn't come. His mother invited me to sit down with her and her daughter and watch TV, but I said I'd wait outside. I waited and waited, but Sid didn't come. I began to get cold from just standing there. I saw Sid's face in an upstairs window, ducking as I glanced up.

But I wouldn't leave.

Finally, reluctantly, Sid stepped outside. I was standing by my pony.

"What are you doing?" he asked, kicking at a chunk of frozen ground. He seemed to have a hard time getting the words out.

I shrugged. I felt a rush of discomfort. I hardly knew why I was there anymore. But then I acted, as if blindly. "Come on," I said. I led my pony across the yard toward the back of the barn.

I felt that I was moving blindly. I didn't know what I was doing. I didn't want to do this. Sid looked worried. He glanced around and followed me, his expression unhappy.

At the back of the barn were stables, facing out to the pasture. I stopped here.

Sid stopped too. He was jittering.

"You know, there are two billion black holes in the universe," he said.

"What's a black hole?" I asked, putting my pony's reins on a hook.

"It's an empty dark hole with nothing in it, no light or air or bottom." He snickered, nervously. " If you fall in, you just disappear."

I stepped toward him. He leaned back away from me, then even stepped backward. His face was scared, cloudy. His back was now pressed against the stable wall.

I was moving without thinking. I leaned up and put my lips on his. He jerked his head back a little. He laughed nervously, looked around. Then, as if he had no other option, he bent near and put his mouth on mine, trying it. His lips were soft. When he brought his face away, his eyes were already different. He came near and kissed me again, then to my surprise, pressed his tongue inside my mouth, at first a little bit, then deeper, then all the way in. I felt something wiggle up from between my legs all the way to my throat.

Afterward, we walked back across the frozen yard, past a pile of old motors. Sid was acting different. He lit a cigarette. His step was jauntier. I felt happier, too. We passed the rose of Sharon bush, now just a skeleton. I pictured how it would be in the summer, bursting with hand-sized purple flowers.

That spring, Bonnie Rider killed herself one morning. She had it all planned in advance, went out by the pond behind her house, tied rocks on her feet, and stepped in. It happened over the weekend. We found out because they announced it over the loudspeaker at school. "We regret to inform you that Bonnie Rider passed away over the weekend."

"'Passed away'?" Trish whispered across the aisle. "What does that mean?"

"Died," I said, though I looked around when saying it because even I wasn't sure.

Four days later, Marcy and Denise decided to do the same. They were on the phone together, both with their fathers' hunting guns in their hands. In the notes they left, they said they "wanted to be with Bonnie." When they weren't on the bus, we thought it was because they were upset about Bonnie. But then the announcement played over the loudspeaker that Marcy was also dead. Denise had decided not to at the last minute.

For a moment, on the bus, the jittering, pulsing, jamming stopped. It actually felt, for a split second, like the end of the world. Then it started again, but differently. Shirley explained in a quiet voice about all the historical figures she knew of who had killed themselves. "Suicide," she explained, "is an ancient practice." Though we'd grown tired of listening to her, we felt in that moment that we'd never been so relieved to hear a person's voice.

*

Summer came and we all still went out riding, we still had a great time. The boys' voices were changing, our breasts were growing, they had more hair in their armpits, yet it was still possible. Jesse was a little different, his face heavier, less angelic-looking. Something really inexplicably bad had happened. The boys lied less. What was the point? Reality this time had outstretched fantasy. We still went to the Lyalls' pool. The boys collected dog turds and put them in people's mailboxes. They knocked over road signs. But things were changing all around us, we were changing. Time was moving forward, we couldn't stop it. Lu and I were going one way, the Kalowski boys the other.

The following year at school, we'd all drift further apart. Lu and Shirley would be waiting for their boy-friends, going out on dates. The Kalowski boys would start committing their first petty crimes. (At one point, there was some suspicion that they'd broken into our house and stolen things: a painting with naked people in it, and a tin of our mother's boyfriend's pot.) And the year after that, Lu and I would change schools. Although our father didn't live with us, our parents still made decisions together. They had decided we should go to a different school, that school wasn't good for us. Our parents were so-called hippies, but they were thinking of our future. They had set aside money for us. My sister and I would go to college, while the Kalowski boys would go on to other things. Since we hardly saw them anymore, we didn't know exactly what, but there were rumors—prison on drug charges, fathering children young.

But we still had this summer. The rose of Sharon bush was now in full bloom. It shed a black shadow on the ground. Sid and I still kissed sometimes in secret behind the barn. I thought a lot about kissing him. His mouth was soft and voluminous. He'd put his finger in my bellybutton. "Give me your tongue," he'd say. In the pasture, out riding, I'd look over at him. Since that day I'd gone to find him, he was different, I could tell. He wasn't so afraid. And I was different too. I knew it. I had a secret. It had nothing to do with anyone, not my parents, not the girls. I was no longer less or the least. I had a secret, out of sight of everyone, blooming inside me. I would carry it with me out into the world.

RETURN

Around the house there are briars with thorns. The goat house has collapsed. The apple trees have grown gray and old. Near them are new ones sprouting, sprigs from the ground. The path down to the pasture that the children used to take is overgrown. No one passes along it anymore. The nettles have grown thick and tall and shiny. The creek has changed its course. The swimming hole—there's still a swimming hole and the children's mother and her husband still swim in it—is in a different place and where it used to be is very shallow. You can see the rocks under the ripples. The house, too, has changed. It has grown rooms and walls, like a crustacean that has added an extra shell.

Their mother's husband has a studio above the house, a new building. They've planted grapes. They have bees. Each time the children—if they can even be called that now—come home, they adjust in their heads where one thing was and another is now. Though their lives have other stories—they have gone away, to college and the world, and come back home and rested in their beds, having long outgrown their beds, and then gone away again— they continue with this story whose existence they haven't ever entirely forgotten. It stirs beneath everything, murmuring, like the undercurrent of the creek.

The house, the old bookshelves, rough slabs of wood nailed to the wall; the books, they remember them, poring through their titles, the set of encyclopedias, the black wig.

All that whispering throughout the house. They remember everything, everything, or nothing at all. They come home, famished. They eat all the food in the kitchen. They try to fit their hulking bodies onto the swing. They play the same games, backgammon, Ping-Pong, cards, smoking now. Or new ones. They talk. They bring friends.

Their mother has kept the house, has kept their old things, in the closets, in boxes. They glance at them, pick through them, terrariums, polished rocks, sticks containing vague memories, holsters, wooden swords. They look through their bureaus at the collections of remnant clothes.

They come home, their mother watches them come home, and then they go away again.

They see their father elsewhere. They make a point of seeing him as he, when they were little, made a point of seeing them. They meet up with him at his storage deposit house, which he still owns. The neighborhood has grown tonier, people even complaining now about his backyard. Or they go to his girlfriend's house. He's back again with a girlfriend he once had, Lonnie, and lives most of the time at her house. Sometimes they see him on trips. He comes to visit them wherever they live. They do the same things with him, ski, go swimming. Sometimes in the car now they're the ones who drive, but he still has theories about absolutely everything and goes on talking his head off on and on.

At home, in the hall closet, they find the old brown soccer ball and try to pump it up. They find the baseball bat, which used to be so heavy. Now it's like a leaf. "Is this a baby bat?" they ask. "Is this regulation size?" They take the soccer ball outside to kick it around in the yard. The house settles. All those big bodies, gone again, thank God.

Though just for a moment. The door opens again. One of them comes back in to get the pump, the ball's still too soft, then goes out again. For a moment now, the rooms are inhabited as they used to be when the children lived here, beds unmade, clothes on the floor. The sink in the bathroom drips. On the counter there are crumbs.

The children do chores; the boys chop wood. Or they drive into town to run errands, buy groceries. They still feel funny when they pass the woman's house with the cats and the clay. Above her is the house where the man who is now their mother's husband used to live with his wife when they were both very young and the children would go there to play.

Certain things make sense now. Others are still baffling. They pick up a book that baffled and intrigued them, D. H. Lawrence's *Sons and Lovers,* and suddenly it makes sense. Suddenly all kinds of things make sense. And others still don't and never will.

Lying in their beds, they feel that unsettled sensation of having grown large in the night. They aren't always sure where the change happened—if they're the ones who've changed or if the place has. They shrink and feel larger.

They can reach up now and pick the fruit off the fruit trees whereas before from the ground it seemed so far away.

They can close the doors to their rooms now—the house, renovated, now has doors—but hide? They still go outside to hide. They walk swiftly, hands in pockets. As they cross the yard, they feel their bodies turning hot and cold, as when they used to swim in the creek and pass through hot and cold spots. They feel frightened, then pleased. They feel a great tenderness for certain things. That was where the goats gathered. That's where the cider press still stands, unused for years. Suddenly they feel enraged. How could things go unused like that for years? They should move back here, settle in, make it all work again, make it all as it was again exactly, replicate that world—but why? It seems to have suddenly slipped their minds that they have whole other worlds and even people waiting for them to return. And even so, why replicate this world that has gone? Because it was so perfect? But it was not. But it was. Perfect because it was the world before the world changed. Any change then becomes a blot of imperfection.

As they walk down the pasture road, their heads swirl with old images, and meanwhile their magic animal bodies remain immune, soak in the sun, rise to the dizzying smell of the honeysuckle, thrown like a blanket over the fence. It seems that these magical animal bodies of theirs just live in the instant, as they always did, now and then, grow dizzy over honeysuckle, soak in the sun, as if nothing has changed, no time ever passed.

Going down the road, the past swirling in their heads, the future rushing headlong into their faces—but whom will they ever meet, whom will they ever know who will take the place of this? Will spots on their skin ever feel so sore because of a recent event, a recent person, that is, a person who is not of this childhood world? Will their dreams ever plunge forward instead of taking them back here? Will they ever recover the whole of their beings, and not have that one part, that little ghost, waiting there at the edge of the yard? That little ghost, look at her, there she stands.

Oh God, forget it. They throw up their hands, shake their heads free of all these images.

"Let's not think of it." One of them is irritated, bored with all this talk. "I don't remember anything!"

Another remembers everything, too much.

"It's invented, that never happened," a third says.

"It did happen. It did!"

"I was too young. I don't remember."

"Too young? But you were fourteen!"

They invent memories. They confuse which thing happened to whom.

"But that wasn't you—that happened to me!"

"No it didn't. Look, I have the scar."

"But I have a scar there too." They stare at each other, eerily.

The pasture, they realize now, is not so far away as they thought it was. They enter it, cross it. The pasture grass is the same. It still blows the same way. They look at the creek. There are the places where the water really shoots down, then the places where it jostles, a silver fiddling lace-like hem, and then there are the deep shining pools. They dip their hands in. They take their boots off and walk in, though it's still cold. Their feet are more tender now than they used to be. They look pink and pale. The stones on the bottom hurt them. They don't remember this feeling. They used to stand and play here for hours. When they look at the photo albums, they're always surprised. That's all they're ever doing, playing and laughing.

They cross the creek and on the other side, stepping out, find a field they've never seen. They squint at it into the light. Was this here all along? they ask. How could they have missed it? The only fields they knew were up on the hill. They question each other. They had thought they knew every part of this land. Now here, so close up, is a glowing field. What else did they miss? What more lies unknown?

They cross back over the creek again and stretch out in the pasture grass. They remember how they used to wish they could be plants and lie very still near the ground all night and in the morning be covered with tears of dew. They think they would still like that. They look up. The grass beneath them is the same, but has renewed itself many times and the sky has passed over a thousand billion times. A buzzard circles. Is it coming for them? They'll lie still this time, they won't move. Always before they were too scared to wait. They'll wait now and see if it really falls. The buzzard hovers, gathers itself. They remember how they've seen the eyes plucked out of things. Then it plummets, plummets straight for their faces. They feel it suddenly very close, hear the rush of wings and sense the sharp beak. They can't wait, they sit up. The buzzard stops, lifts, strays. It wasn't as close as they'd thought after all. They remain there sitting and watch it veer away.

Would it be possible to begin all over again? Start again. Relive things.

"What would be the point?" one of them says. "Let's just forget it."

They throw a rock into the stream. But it's that the body remembers, like those warm and cold spots they feel crossing the yard.

They go into the woods. Or up onto the hill where the fields they always knew begin. They discover that the fields that spread out at the top of the mountain are the same fields you pass if you drive along the road on the way to the bus stop, a connection they had never made.

And the world out there? Are they liking it? They've had some adventures. And love? Yes, love, too, they know something about that, they've fallen in love.

"You have?"

"Really?"

They look at one another, discovering in each other their own gestures. There just now is how their father wobbles his hand, and there the way their mother squints. It makes them laugh. Seeing each other again, in general, makes them laugh. It's as if they'd forgotten each other for a moment somewhere along the line, in trying to be themselves, detached, single beings in the world, and now here they are again, together, the children.

They're with each other, older now, going down to the pasture, kicking at stones, laughing, some of them smoking. One leaps on another's back. Look at them, the children, gathered in a group. The girls and the boys. You can see them if you look down from the kitchen windows. It's all just beginning, their lives are just beginning. Who knows what awaits them?

The dust begins to settle. Soon now they'll scatter, returning to their worlds.

They go outside together or else, while the others are all doing something, cleaning up a meal, playing Ping-Pong in the basement, they go out on their own, adults now—or almost—hands in pockets, they walk out into the yard. The amazing thing is that it's still here. It's all still here. Oh, with the changes, of course. They pass a spot, beneath the cherry trees—something happened there, what was it? They're not sure. A feeling of their bodies pressing into the grass. And then they look up at the trees themselves, so much bigger now. They remember how they played in them, up in the branches, they spent their whole lives there, how they pressed their faces into showers of leaves. They walk out farther, toward the edge of the yard, where the berry bushes used to grow. There's a bench there now, their mother's husband's contribution. They sit for a moment, looking out at the road. It was there, in that spot, not far from the mailbox, where I once stood at a terrible loss.

For I was one of those children and now, hands in my pockets, whistling a little tune, I pick myself up and stroll away.

Acknowledgments

Many grateful acknowledgments go to Sarah Chalfant and Sarah McGrath, to readers Juan Pablo Domenech and Mary Gordon, consultants Clover Swann, Mary Swann, and Leda Swann, and the people who gave me places to write: Henry Greenwalt, Horacio Kaufmann, Debi and Guntram Hapsburg, and the Ingram and Mueenuddin families.

About the Author

Maxine Swann has been awarded *Ploughshares'* Cohen Award for best fiction of the year, an O. Henry Award, and a Pushcart Prize, and her work has been included twice in *The Best American Short Stories* selection (1998, 2006). Her first novel, *Serious Girls,* was published in 2003. She has lived in Paris and Pakistan and now lives in Buenos Aires.